Reservoir
Road
Adventure

Reservoir Road Adventure

Erna M. Holyer

BAKER BOOK HOUSE
Grand Rapids, Michigan 49506

ISBN: 0-8010-4261-5

Contents

Spanish/English Translations

sí	yes
ah, sí?	oh, yes?
hermano	brother
verdad?	isn't that true?
verdad!	it is true
es verdad?	is it true?
está buen	it is all right
adiós	good-by
Señora, señora	Mrs., lady
niños	children
gracias	thanks, thank you
hermana	sister
muchas gracias	many thanks
momentino	one small moment

chapter ONE

Company Coming

The California canyon drowsed in the noon sun. Live oaks and bay trees spread green umbrellas over cottages. The little houses rose from the creekbed on stilty legs.

A mail truck broke the stillness. Dogs barked and squirrels scolded. The postman stopped in the hamlet. Mailboxes clustered in the town's center.

A boy came running. Dark hair bounced on his forehead. White teeth flashed in his brown face. "Have you got mail for Morales?" he called. The postman sorted bundles in the truck. "What's your number?"

"This is our box, see?" the boy pointed.

The postman pulled out a letter. "Rolando Morales, is that you?"

"It's my papa. I am Daniel." The boy ran off, waving the letter. At a flimsy bridge, he opened the gate. His family lived in a rented cabin. Moss crept over the house and leaves littered the roof.

"Papa, Mamma, Linda, Angelina!"

Daniel burst into the kitchen. Four glad faces crowded around him.

Papa pulled a note from the envelope. "Looks like it is from Felix," he ventured.

Mamma leaned over his shoulder. "What does your brother write?"

Daniel knew Papa couldn't read, but he wouldn't hurt Papa's pride. He handed the note to Daniel. "Read it aloud, son."

"I will try, Papa." Daniel studied the scrawl without hurry. A field worker had written the note for his uncle, who couldn't write. Finally, Daniel announced, "They are coming."

Papa looked embarrassed. "Who is coming?"

"Uncle Felix and his family."

"Does the letter say when they are coming?" Papa asked.

Daniel nodded. *"Si,* on Monday."

Papa put his arm around Mamma. Her moon-shaped face was tense.

"Which Monday, son?" Papa asked.

"Second Monday in June." Daniel noticed that Mamma looked half-sick.

"June is now and this is Monday," Mamma exclaimed. "Are they coming *today*?" Papa's rough hand gently touched her forehead. "Better read it again, son."

"Second Monday in June." Daniel made certain there was no mistake.

Mamma fumbled with the collar of her

faded dress. She was breathing hard. "We need food. We must cook," she gasped. "Why did they write so late, Daniel?"

"Uncle Felix had to find somebody in a labor camp who'd write the letter for him," Daniel explained. "He didn't know we moved. The letter went to our old address in New Almaden first."

Mamma's face looked sallow. Papa eased her onto a seat. He spoke gently. "I will bring flour and beans. Linda and Daniel will clean the cabin and watch Angelina. You rest." Papa led Mamma to the bedroom. "If you rest now, you may feel fine later," he told Mamma.

Back in the kitchen, Papa put a wide-brimmed straw hat onto his shock of black hair. Across the creek, he started the pickup truck and roared off.

Before long, Papa was back with food. Linda and Daniel worked together, cooking, cleaning, and laughing. Mamma caught their joy and left her bed. Beans soon bubbled on the gas flame and tortillas made a stack on the table. Papa again donned his hat. "I will wait for Felix at the old address," he explained.

Daniel left the stove. "Let me come with you, Papa."

"No, Daniel. Mamma needs you. Better stay here." Papa looked sorry. Daniel pushed the broom, washed the window, and kept little Angelina from getting underfoot. Mamma's smile kept him on the job. Linda's dazzling grins helped too. Two years younger than Daniel, the eleven-year-old was helping her mother all she could.

Done with his chores, Daniel hoisted Angelina on his shoulders. He raced her around in the yard. The three-year-old was light as a feather. Linda had slicked stubborn ringlets from the child's face and tied curly strands with yellow ribbons.

Angelina's giggling suddenly stopped. A pickup truck whirled up dust beside the creek. It stopped and parked. Daniel called into the kitchen.

"Uncle Felix is here!"

Angelina kicked to get away. Daniel pressed her close. "Don't be afraid. It's only the relatives," he soothed. "They are not strangers."

Truck doors slammed and the bridge swayed. People Daniel faintly remembered walked through the gate. "Is this you, Daniel?" they asked. "Is this Baby Angelina?" "Where is Linda?" "Where is your mamma?" "We met your papa. He'll come as soon as he gets the motor started."

The relatives all spoke at once. They hugged and kissed and carried on. It was like rain showers from blue skies, like sunshine from clouds. Daniel felt confused. Angelina screamed as she was being passed from one pair of affectionate arms to another.

Around the Moraleses' makeshift table, Daniel got reacquainted with the relatives. Papa's older brother was broad-shouldered, stocky, and husky like Papa. And he boasted the same comfortable laugh. Aunt Lupe was a plain, heavy-set woman. Lupe's mother, Rosita, had gray streaks in her formerly jet-black hair. Gilbert, nineteen, and Emilio, seventeen, had grown into handsome lads.

Daniel suspected the cousins would soon look for wives, for migrants married early. Even so, the cousins were bashful. Daniel guessed they felt embarrassed about their changed voices.

The relatives were happy as children to find Daniel's family tucked away in that green canyon. Daniel felt taken back to times past, before Mamma's open-heart surgery. His family had harvested crops in California's sun-drenched valleys and spent the winter months in Arizona. The past year scaled away. Daniel was a carefree boy again. The relatives had not meant so much then. They had been around like sunshine and rain. Now he felt like he had found lost friends—friends who understood as only family could understand. Friends who sympathized because they, too, were struggling.

Granny Rosita watched the lips of everybody. Uncle Felix explained, "Rosita has a hard time in the field now. When the row boss yells, she cannot hear him. Then somebody gives her the signal to hurry up." Uncle Felix drew a deep breath. "Rosita is going deaf. Pretty soon she won't be able to work anymore."

Daniel noticed deep sorrow in his uncle's sun-browned face. Poor Rosita, she was so loving, outgoing toward everybody. Daniel remembered times when Rosita and Mamma cooked meals for huge family gatherings. Rosita cooked the best food this side of Mexico. Everybody said so. Now she couldn't hear. Rosita had brought a "package of love" for Mamma. Mamma opened the package, saying Rosita shouldn't have spent the money, but she slipped on the red sandals with great pleasure. It was good hearing old names again. Smells, people, and songs flashed through Daniel's mind. Forgotten sensations rushed back as the relatives brought Papa and Mamma up to date on family happenings.

Suddenly stillness fell over the group of people in the little shack. Then everybody cried. Rosita's husband, Alfredo, had passed away. Poor Alfredo, he had been such a good man! Poor Rosita, she was now a widow! Daniel's head swam, he felt so sorry for her.

"Alfredo never complained," Rosita was

saying. "He knew he was dying, but he put his faith in the Lord." Her look told Daniel that Rosita had seen bad sights, felt bad feelings. She no longer was the laughing woman Daniel remembered. She looked older and stranger. Daniel joined the family in hugging and comforting her. It was all he could do to make her feel better.

And Rosita responded to their love. "Let us no longer cry over the dead," she said. "Let us not worry about my going deaf. Main thing I can still work. When we find a good camp, perhaps Felix will take me to a doctor." She brightened. "Felix has been a wonderful son-in-law. I am so lucky Lupe married a good man who takes care of me in my old days."

Lupe interrupted her mother. "Felix is used to looking after everybody. He is the oldest in the Morales family."

Uncle Felix interrupted. "Enough talk about me." Facing Papa, he said, "What is happening with you, Rolando? Why did you move from New Almaden? Was that village not closer to the place of your work?"

Papa's Adam's apple moved up and down. He did not relish talking about troubles. "The construction boss laid me off," he said. "Times are bad. Many good men are out of work."

Before Papa confessed just how bad things stood with the family, Daniel spoke up. "The landlord put us out, Uncle Felix. This house is cheap. And it's good for Mamma. The trees make it cool and let her heart pump better."

"How is your dear mother?" Aunt Lupe interrupted.

"I am fine, thank you." Mamma spoke for herself. "At the hospital where they gave me the valve, the doctors said I am fine."

"She must go for a checkup in October," Papa added. "She must exercise and watch her diet. And she must not do heavy work, lifting and such. It's no problem. The children help around the house."

Mamma smiled. "I never had it so good, Lupe. I have a home. I can stay inside when I please."

"Ah, si?" Aunt Lupe frowned. "How long can you pay rent when nobody works?" she wanted to know.

Uncle Felix gave his wife a disapproving look. "Quiet, woman! Rolando will find work, won't you, *hermano?*" He slapped Papa's shoulder. His laugh erased the shadows on Papa's outdoor face. Uncle Felix was a happy kind of man. When crinkles webbed his eyes, everybody brightened.

Daniel admired his uncle. There was a man who managed to deal with people, Daniel thought. Uncle Felix caught his glance.

"And what is new with you, Daniel?" Uncle Felix asked.

"Nothing much," Daniel stuttered.

Papa urged, "Go, get your spectacles, son." Turning to his brother, Papa added, "This boy is smart, Felix. Next year he will move up to grade six. Not bad for a migrant boy, eh?"

Daniel fetched the hated glasses. When they straddled his nose, Papa tapped his chest with pride. "Rolando Morales, he now has a son who is a student, *verdad?*"

"Verdad." The relatives contemplated Daniel with awe.

"Who knows," Papa gloated, "Daniel may be the first boy in the family to earn a high school diploma."

"A high school diploma?" Aunt Lupe exclaimed. "Gilbert and Emilio are helping to feed the family. What good is sitting in school?"

Linda spoke without being asked. "We learn useful things which will help us later, Aunt Lupe. Daniel can read better than anybody in the family. Our teachers say children who study hard can find good jobs when they grow up."

Papa sided with Linda. "Daniel's teacher tells me my son is smart. She even calls him a naturalist."

"A what?" The cousins' mouths fell open.

Linda answered for Papa. "A naturalist is somebody who studies nature."

"What a foolish thing!" Aunt Lupe raised her voice. "Nature is there and that is that."

"Quiet, woman!" Uncle Felix hushed his wife. "Young people can do worse things, drinking, gambling, smoking, for example."

The cousins elbowed each other. "Or getting started on dope," they grinned. Aunt Lupe's stern glance made them look guilty. She pointed at Angelina, who clung to Mamma. "Why is this baby scared?"

Mamma put protective arms around the girl. "She has always been like this; she cannot help it."

"She has not spoken one word since we arrived," Aunt Lupe continued.

Linda rushed to her sister's defense. "Angelina can speak lots of words."

"Such as?" Aunt Lupe pinned her down.

Linda squirmed. "She doesn't have to *speak*. We always understand what she wants."

"Ah, sí?" Aunt Lupe gave Uncle Felix a strange look.

Mamma rose from the fruit crate which served as a chair in the Morales household. "Come, Linda, help me get dinner ready."

Bean-filled tortillas and strawberries from the relatives' last place of work could have made a family feast. But the women did not speak much and Daniel's glasses got steamed up.

The families bedded down in the crowded cabin. Daniel heard voices in the yard before daybreak. What made Papa and Uncle Felix get up so early, he wondered?

chapter two

Family Breakup

Mamma stirred on the bed's far side. "Who is out there?" she whispered.

"Papa and Uncle Felix," Daniel whispered back.

Mamma sounded alarmed. "Why don't you see what the men are up to," she suggested.

Daniel darted into his jeans. He had slept in the big bed so Granny Rosita got a good night's sleep in his bed. Linda and Angelina breathed quietly beside Mamma. Daniel tiptoed through the kitchen. The door creaked as he opened it.

"Is that you, Daniel?" Papa asked.

"*Sí.*"

"What do you want, son?"

"I cannot sleep, Papa."

"Might as well hear the news," said Papa. "Uncle Felix wants us to come with him."

"*Es verdad?* When do we leave?" Excitement rushed through the boy.

"Soon. Help us get the pickup ready."

"*Sí!*" Daniel turned on the yard light. He helped the men to mount pipes and canvas on Papa's truck. When everything was rigged up, Papa tousled Daniel's head.

"Está buen, son. We'll load the rest after breakfast. Go, wake up those sleepyheads.''

Breakfast brought surprises. When everybody sat around the table, Linda glimpsed the pickup through the window. "What's the canvas for?" she screeched.

Daniel broke the news: "We're going after the crops again."

"Not me!" Linda exploded. "I want to stay. I want a home like Mrs. Henderson, clean clothes, and a bathtub. Let others pick beans and berries and tomatoes. I want a bed for my babies when I grow up."

"Linda, bite your tongue!" In all his life, Daniel had not seen his sister so disrespectful. Without her grin, the eleven-year-old reminded him of somber Aunt Lupe.

"I'm not leaving," Linda declared. "People have been good to us. This canyon is a fine place to live."

Aunt Lupe's lips curled. "Live among Anglo people? To Anglos you're nothing but a Mexican kid, a Chicano, a migrant."

"Mrs. Henderson says Mexican-American kids have the same rights as Anglo children. They can attend school and live in houses."

"And who is Mrs. Henderson?" A deep line furrowed Aunt Lupe's sun-darkened forehead.

"She is the woman I work for sometimes.

13

She has a baby and a poodle. She lets me take care of them in her house while she works." Linda spoke with pride.

Papa soothed the girl. "It is true, Linda, the people of New Almaden have been good to us. We are grateful. The town is a fine place, but your mother needs you. She cannot work in the fields no more. The doctors laid the law down. 'Mr. Morales,' they said, 'field work is out for your wife. Exercise yes, hard work no.' "

"Work is better than exercise," Aunt Lupe suggested. "When she gets tired, she can rest in the pickup."

Papa looked troubled. "If she gets sick, she may be too far from the hospital where they gave her the valve. What do we do if she needs help?"

Daniel munched on his food while the adults talked about the problem. The relatives talked this way. Papa talked that way. Everybody tried to find a solution. Daniel yearned to travel with Papa. School was out and there was nothing to do in the little settlement of Twin Creek where they lived.

Linda wanted to stay. Mamma wanted to go with Papa. Angelina cried and clung to Daniel, still mistaking the relatives for strangers. Did Papa himself want to go? Uncle Felix was Papa's oldest brother. The oldest male in the family decided. It was the rule. Uncle Felix commanded respect.

Then the final word was spoken: Papa would accompany Uncle Felix and share the pickup with Gilbert and Emilio. Mamma, Linda, and Angelina were to stay at the cabin. And Daniel? The boy waited for the verdict.

"Daniel, you stay here," Papa decided. "Look after Mamma and your sisters, and keep yourself out of trouble."

Turning to Mamma, Papa added, "I will send money if I can. Be good and don't work hard."

Not working hard was a luxury in a migrant family. But then, they weren't migrants any longer, or were they, Daniel wondered? Papa had found jobs as a gas station attendant, janitor, and cement finisher. He had been fired from the gas station the day Mamma was ill and he stayed by her side. He had quit the janitorial job when the boss of the cement finishers offered him more money. And he had been out of work since the January rains, six months ago. Whatever their status, Daniel resolved to seek work and help Papa out. It would be the next thing to helping the family in the fields.

Papa's eyes shimmered as he hugged the children and embraced Mamma to say *adiós*. Before boosting his stocky frame into the cab, he repeated to Daniel, "Look out for Mamma and your sisters, and keep yourself out of trouble."

"I will do that," Daniel promised.

Papa seemed relieved. *Está buen,* he said. "I will return for Mamma's checkup in October. You are now the man of the family, Daniel. Take care until I come back."

Papa joined the cousins in the cab. Uncle Felix, his wife, and Granny Rosita sat in the other truck. Everyone waved. Engines started up. Headlights glared in the dawn. And Papa followed his brother down the dead-end street.

Daniel held his screaming little sister. Mamma was crying. She wanted to go with Papa, rather than live without him. The family was torn apart. Daniel kicked at pebbles.

"What a fool I am," he scolded himself. "Why did I not tear up that letter? Why did I not toss it into the creek?" Filled with regrets, he led his charges back to the cabin.

In the windowless porch that held his bed, Daniel turned on the light. The bird book that his elderly friend, Mr. Randall, had given him did not cheer him today.

Why did the relatives whisk Papa away? Things had been bad enough. Why this change for the worse?

The sun climbed over the trees, but the cabin remained dark. The kitchen window looked gloomy, despite the frilly curtains Linda and Mamma had made for it. Daniel missed the sounds of working people. He turned to his sister.

"What are you doing, Linda?"

"Nothing much. Why?"

"Let's go down to the village."

"What for?" Linda put the pots and pans she had been scrubbing into a fruit-crate cupboard.

"Look for work. You haven't seen Mrs. Henderson since we moved. Ask if she needs you again."

"O.K.!" Linda parted her brown hair in the center. Straightening her blouse, she presented herself to Mamma. "Do I look nice?" she asked. Mamma smiled.

"You always look nice, Linda. Tell *Señora* Henderson our man is traveling also." Mamma was referring to Mr. Henderson, whose job as a salesman kept him on the road.

"Will you be all right?" Linda asked.

"*Sí.* I will put Angelina to bed and rest myself. The night was short." She hugged Linda and tousled Daniel's hair. "Do not worry about me, *niños.* God will keep me safe."

Brother and sister headed for the paved road that snaked along a ravine that drained foothills in the Pacific Coast Range. Winter rains had filled this reservoir, but by late summer it would be dry.

Leaning fence posts strung with barbed wire made crooked lines along the road. Wildflowers dotted the bank. Birds twittered in oak trees and a ground squirrel whistled near its burrow.

Across the water, cows lowed in hillside pastures and calves answered back.

Brother and sister walked in silence. Rays of sun broke through the mist, sparkling on glass splinters on the road and on the dew-fresh faces of poppies and lupines. Daniel thought it was a magic world they had entered, a world of beauty and peace.

Suddenly a car roared up from behind. Daniel pulled Linda onto the gravel bank. The car whizzed past. Teen-agers yelled and threw out a bottle. A second car squealed around the curve. It speeded past, tires squealing.

Daniel pulled Linda from the stinging wire. Linda rubbed her arm.

"Have I dreamed a bad dream, or is this a racetrack, Daniel?"

Daniel felt troubled. Birds still sang and the road looked peaceful. But it was not the same. Cows stood on the hillside, white faces turned toward the road, poised to run. When Daniel gently called to them, they stampeded.

Linda walked ahead. She stopped by a signpost. Neck craned, she called, "Look,

Daniel, see if you can make sense of this." She read haltingly, "God made man. Man made grass. Grass made high."

Daniel squinted. He had left his glasses at home. "Warning! Do not swim in these waters!" he read aloud.

"That's the big letters, Daniel. Read the writing *people* made."

"Let's not read nonsense," Daniel suggested.

Suddenly Linda balked. "I'm afraid, Daniel. There are bad people on this road."

Daniel took his sister's hand. "You needn't be afraid, Linda. I'll protect you."

Then the town's little church peeked through huge eucalyptus trees downhill. Daniel and Linda entered a tree-shaded road and climbed the path to the Henderson house. A black poodle yipped behind the window, looking like a toy.

A slender woman was carrying a crying toddler to the compact car out front. She strapped the little one into the seat.

"Mrs. Henderson!" Linda called out.

Dimples showed in the woman's face. "Linda, how good to see you!"

"I can work for you again, Mrs. Henderson. We are now settled."

"When can you start?"

"Right now!"

The pale woman frowned. "I must make

arrangements with the nursery, Linda. They've been taking care of Junior. Can you come tomorrow morning?''

"*Sí.* Do you want me to come every day?''

"We'll work that out tomorrow, Linda. Come early, for I mustn't be late for work.'' She backed out of the flat spot and slithered downhill.

Linda tapped the windowpane and baby-talked with the poodle. Daniel touched her shoulder. "Let us not waste time, Linda. Let us find a job and earn money today.''

"I have a job, starting tomorrow.'' Linda looked surprised.

"We can both ask for work today, Linda. Maybe somebody needs clean windows,'' Daniel urged.

Linda sat down on the porch step. "I am tired, Daniel. We must have walked a couple miles.''

"It was nothing compared to the stooping we used to do in the field,'' Daniel countered.

"I want to go home,'' Linda pouted.

"You are getting soft, Linda. You can sit here all day while I look for work.''

"Be here alone?'' Linda's eyes snapped.

"Nobody is going to hurt you here in town.''

"I want to go home!''

chapter three

A Strange Sergeant

Daniel remembered his promise to Papa, to look out for his sister. He guided Linda home over the hot and glaring reservoir road, and cooled his feet in the creek at home. He did not want to share the cabin with Linda. But when she called him for lunch, he forgot to be angry with her.

Daniel accompanied Linda again the next morning. The manmade lake lay still and dark. Mourning doves called in the dewy freshness, and a few approaching cars soon clanked over the cattle guard on the side road. The side road led to an Air Force base high on Hummingbird Mountain.

A truck pulling a horse trailer stopped beside the youngsters.

"Have you kids seen any cattle outside the fence?" the rancher asked.

"No. What should we do if we see any?" Daniel asked.

"Tell the postmaster, O.K.?"

"O.K."

"Thanks, boy." The rancher drove off.

Linda pointed to the pavement. "Look at this ugly thing, Daniel!"

Daniel squinted. He wished he had brought his glasses. Stooping, he saw with alarm the form of a twisted toad. The dead creature brought tears to his eyes.

"Poor little toad," Daniel sobbed. "I wish I could have helped you." Walking on, he muttered, "Drivers killed it. They went too fast and couldn't stop."

"It was only a toad." Linda spoke lightly.

"And who says that toads are worth less than other creatures?"

"It would have died anyway."

"It wouldn't have died now," Daniel countered. "It was migrating to the water to lay its eggs. Now there won't be many polliwogs. The driver killed the toad's children also."

"What happens when there aren't any more toads? What are toads good for anyway?"

"They catch lots of bugs. Besides, when one animal species dies out, other creatures suffer a loss too." Daniel recalled the teacher's lesson.

"Verdad?" Linda made a somber face. She was thinking, Daniel knew. On the dam's turnout, she lingered.

"Move on, Linda!" Daniel passed the litter-strewn turnaround. Blue jays screeched in the canyon below and quail scurried into underbrush.

White road markers and yellow reflectors warned drivers of dangerous curves. The right shoulder dropped off to a tangle of bay trees, alders, and oaks. Alamitos Creek chattered below. The left shoulder wound itself around the rocks from which the road was cut. Shattered glass spoke of windshield-breaking accidents.

Daniel whisked Linda up the side road that climbed to the Henderson house. He waited until the women settled Linda's working schedule. Linda came bouncing out of the front door. Her cheeks, like sausages, bulged under her dancing eyes.

"I won't come home tonight," Linda reported. "Mrs. Henderson will drive me home Friday. She wants me to come every Monday morning. Imagine, I can stay all week and get my meals!"

"How much money does she pay you?"

"Five dollars a week."

"Ask her if she will give you ten."

"But, Daniel!" Linda gasped.

"It's only two dollars a day. You are worth that much. Tell her we need the money." Daniel was firm.

"Oh, Daniel!" Linda shuffled into the house. Soon she returned, looking dazed. "I got it, Daniel! Mrs. Henderson was not mad at me for asking."

"See!" Daniel hummed all the way down to Main Street. He emptied Mr. Randall's mailbox and took the mail to his friend's door. The drapes were drawn and all was quiet inside. Daniel thought his elderly friend was sleeping. Mr. Randall was not as strong as he used to be. Walking put more strain on the heavy man than ever before.

Daniel left town. Bright sunlight dazzled him in the valley. He entered the suburbs of the great city of San Jose. At the first traffic signal, he turned into a housing development and started to ring doorbells. Children opened the doors and sometimes a woman came out. Daniel rattled off his services.

"Do you need lawn cutting? Digging or planting in the yard? Window washing or other odd jobs done?"

"Sorry, we hired a teen-ager." "Sorry, my husband does that." "Sorry, but no." The replies varied, but the answer was no.

Daniel's feet burned and his stomach growled. In the yard of a nearby high school, he found a water fountain and cooled off by the lockers. Teen-agers attending summer school had tossed good food into the garbage cans. Daniel picked out a grapefruit, half a sandwich, and a broken bag of popcorn.

Refreshed, Daniel rang more doorbells. Lucky teen-agers had tied up all the jobs.

Daniel turned back, empty-handed. Hummingbird Mountain with its antenna on top showed him the way. In New Almaden, Daniel walked under tall sycamore trees. He passed cottages overgrown with greenery, the burned-out old post office, and the postal trailer.

At town's end, a highway bridge curved up to the first sharp turn of Reservoir Road. Above the bridge, Daniel hugged the road's edge. An Air Force bus forced him into the foliage. Rushing air pressed against him as the bus passed. Stepping back onto the pavement, Daniel glimpsed fresh tire tracks. Burned rubber told a wild story. A car apparently had raced downhill, hit the cliff, glanced off, swerved across the road, scraped a tree, and hurtled over the bank.

Daniel parted the branches. Squinting, he spotted an upside-down car in the creekside weeds. The wheels were still spinning! Daniel raced back to the post office. Inside, he gasped, "A car went over the bank, right after the bridge. There may be people in it who need help!"

The postmaster lifted up the telephone. "I'll take care of it, Daniel. The firemen will be out in a jiffy."

"Gracias." Daniel raced back and slid down on the bank's loose gravel. He pushed aside the mat of weeds, trying to see inside the car.

"Is anybody in there?" Daniel called.

Moaning sounds answered. Daniel peeked through the tangle of lupines and vines. Three fellows sprawled inside the car. One wore a uniform jacket with sergeant's stripes. He motioned for Daniel to open the door.

Daniel pulled at the handle. It was stuck. He tried the other side. It was blocked by a gravel heap.

"I cannot get the doors open," Daniel called into the cracked window. "But don't you worry. Help is on the way."

"What kind of help?"

"The postmaster called the fire station. The firemen will be here soon."

The uniformed man squeezed a small package through the crack. Daniel thought the sergeant might be stationed at the Air Force base.

"Hey, kid, keep that for me."

"What's in it?" Daniel asked.

"Classified matter. Very important military secret. Nobody must know about it."

"What do you want me to do with it?"

"Don't show it to anybody until I get it back."

Daniel hesitated. The sergeant pushed a five-dollar bill through the crack. "It's yours. Take it and march off!"

Daniel felt unsure about accepting the money. He'd ask Mamma if it was all right to keep it.

The fire truck jangled up the road. Daniel would have liked to see how the men were being helped, but he remembered Mamma and how she sometimes worried about him.

The turnaround was clean this time! Green bags squatted beside the garbage cans. Somebody had picked up the litter.

Daniel felt the package in his pocket. It was taped shut. He was glad he could help somebody. The package made him feel important. A military secret was something that mattered to the country. And Mamma could give the five dollars to the landlord.

When Daniel told her, Mamma shook her head. "When somebody needs help, we must give it, Daniel. When somebody's life is in danger, we must help for free."

"*Si*, Mamma." Daniel felt ashamed. If the doctors had not helped Mamma at the hospital, she might not be alive.

"I'll give the money back," Daniel promised.

Mamma hugged him. "I am proud of you, son. You always have been such a good boy."

Daniel rubbed his face against Mamma's long, black hair. He thanked God that his mother was alive.

Next time Daniel headed for Reservoir Road, he carried the five dollars and the sergeant's package with him. He even carried his glasses, so he would not miss the sergeant.

The glasses let Daniel see everything in sharp focus. Light danced on the water, making a string of diamonds that glittered from shore to shore, pretty as a spider's web.

A duck swam on the water. It was a male, for its voice was faint. The drake raised himself, shook his feathers, then turned in circles. A picture of joy, he floated high, showing off his white neck.

A female duck quacked loudly in the backwater. The drake listened to her call and paddled toward her. She flew out and joined him. Suddenly the pair broke from the surface and flew away. Daniel guessed they had seen him.

Daniel was glad the glasses let him see better, and yet he hated them. Papa had burst with pride when the optometrist fitted his son with the glasses.

"You must take good care of these fine spectacles," Papa had stressed. "No Morales kid ever got something so special."

Papa's joy had found no echo in Daniel. His life had taken a turn for the worse when the optometrist put the strange things on his nose. Daniel thought he must be the only Mexican-American boy with a studious look about him. Why did his eyes have to change? Why couldn't things stay the same?

The ducks flew back and settled on the water. Side by side, they resembled a married couple. Daniel sighed. If only Papa and Mamma could be together. Why the family breakup? Change sat like a sack of beans on Daniel's shoulders. Would the family ever be together again? Mamma had faith in God.

How could you get such faith, Daniel wondered?

Screaming tires alerted Daniel. A jalopy careened into the turnout ahead, churning up dust. A man and a pencil-thin youth jumped out. The driver stayed inside the car and kept the motor running.

chapter four

Sheriff on Horseback

The man and the pencil-thin youth slit open the plastic sacks beside the garbage cans. The two rummaged in the sacks, tossing out bits and pieces. The youth pulled out a can, opened it, and shouted, "I've got it!"

Both jumped into the jalopy and roared toward Daniel. Brakes screeched. The man yelled out the window, "Hey, kid, got my package?"

"W-what?" Daniel barely recognized the sergeant. Yellow stubble bristled on the red face. Shreds of skin marched over nose and forehead to an island of hair that perched high on top of his head. Ice-blue eyes darted beneath the white brows, making Daniel shiver. Despite the stripes on his sleeves, the sergeant did not look like a military man, Daniel decided.

"Gimme my package, kid."

"Y-yes, sir." Daniel produced package and money. "Please take the five dollars back," he said.

The thin teen-ager who sat between the sergeant and the black-bearded driver snapped, "Sarge told you to keep the money. Don't you understand?"

"Y-yes, sir." Daniel handed over the sealed package. The driver revved the motor and took off. Daniel stuffed the money back into his pocket. The encounter left him dazed.

Blue jays screeched in the canyon and the plop of horses' hooves sounded on the road. To Daniel's right, a young man rode up. Dressed in blue denim, he sat astride a chestnut horse whose star shone in the morning sun. To Daniel's left, a blondish horse carried a burly, middle-aged man. Daniel stepped aside as the riders came into view.

"Good morning," Daniel offered. He could not miss the sheriff's badge on the man's chest. The sheriff returned a half-hearted greeting. Riding hard against the shoulder, he kept looking over the bank. Daniel called politely, "Are you looking for something, sir?"

"No, just riding." The sheriff never turned his eyes from the bank. The younger rider scanned the opposite bank with equal concentration. Both men were looking for something important, Daniel guessed. Not wanting to appear curious, he lingered by a corral fence. A fat white mare stood in the enclosure. She looked sluggish and did not react to Daniel's coaxing. The riders disappeared up the road.

A horse trailer was hitched to a car that was parked in the church's parking lot. Scattered straw and fresh droppings littered the ground. The sheriff and his helper had driven to New Almaden, unloaded the horses, and mounted them by the church. What mystery lay up that road, Daniel wondered?

Before turning into Bertram Road, Daniel lifted his chin. A hummingbird hovered between eucalyptus branches, wings ashimmer. Sunlight burst through a stained-glass window, rivaling the bird in beauty. Daniel loved the church with its fragrant trees. It was a place where even the birds praised God.

Daniel scaled the hill to the Henderson house. Mrs. Henderson was leaving for work. Daniel let the car pass. The poodle yipped and Linda dashed out.

"Imagine, Daniel, police found narcotics near the old mine last night. It was on television."

"Where did they find them?" Daniel asked.

"In a rusty old car that went over the bank years ago."

"What do narcotics look like?" Daniel wanted to know.

"Like sugar or flour maybe." Linda turned toward the house. The toddler was screaming. At the door, she looked back. "I'll be home tonight, Daniel."

"I know. It's Friday." Daniel plodded out into the valley and offered his services. The job hunt seemed futile as catching a hummingbird in flight. The sun rode into the dome of the blue sky and dipped to the mountains. Daniel turned homeward. He was hot and hungry.

In town, Daniel checked on Mr. Randall. The old man's face was not as pink as it used to be, but his voice was still brisk. "Good to see you, Daniel. Have you heard from your father yet?"

"No, Mr. Randall. Can I get something for you?"

"Not today, Daniel, thank you. About your father, I'm sure he'll write as soon as he can. Do you miss him?"

"Uh-huh." Daniel hung his head. "I've been job hunting out in the valley. But I haven't made any money yet."

"You must keep up your faith, Daniel. Something will turn up. Wait, don't rush off yet!"

Mr. Randall went into the kitchen. Daniel studied a framed poem, or was it a prayer? It had long and difficult words in it. Daniel could not understand the words, much less remember them. Mr. Randall came back and handed him a plump red apple.

"Thank you, Mr. Randall!" Hungry though he was, Daniel did not eat the apple. He saved it for Angelina.

At town's end, the horse trailer no longer stood by the church. Burned-out flares, dirt, and dry weeds showed where the sergeant's car had been dragged up the road.

Daniel found the rusty jalopy Linda had seen on television. Daniel felt for the five-dollar bill in his pocket. He wished the sergeant had taken it back.

The reservoir's upper region was going dry. Mud shimmered in the bottom. Weeds sprouted around the mud, and along the bank new wildflowers started to bloom. Daniel picked tiny, daisy-like flowers on long stems. He sniffed. The bunch would cheer Mamma.

Twin Creek sweltered in the evening heat. Retired folk cooled off near the creek. The old people lived in neat cottages. Other cottages, unpainted ones, were rented by Twin Creek's bachelors. Nobody was near these cheap places. The bachelors were still on the road, out in the valley somewhere.

Angelina greeted Daniel at the gate. She lifted her little arms to him, making happy noises. Daniel boosted her on his arm, careful not to break the flowers.

Daniel bounced the giggling girl into the house and greeted his mother. "These flowers are for you, Mamma." He sat

Angelina down and gave her the apple. The flowers he carried to the window, so Mamma could appreciate their beauty. She broke off one tiny blossom.

"This flower is a tea," Mamma stated. "Can you bring more, Daniel? The tea is good for the stomach and good for sleep."

"*Si,* Mamma, I can bring all you want." Daniel looked out the window. Linda was leaving Mrs. Henderson's car. She dashed over the bridge, and burst into the kitchen, carrying a brown sack.

"I am home!" Linda beamed.

"Oh, Linda!" Mamma hugged the girl as if she had been away for a year. Linda pulled eight dollars from her jeans.

"Look, Mamma! I made money this week and Mrs. Henderson gave me food from her table. See?" She held the sack so Mamma could see the contents. At the refrigerator, Linda sniffed. "Is the power off, Mamma?"

"*Si,* Linda. We have no money to pay the bill."

"But we have eight dollars. We can have it turned on again."

"Eight dollars are not enough, Linda. Perhaps we have more money next week. Daniel is looking for jobs."

"But this food will go to waste. Everything is melting," Linda wailed. She carried dripping ice trays to the sink. "Help me, Daniel! The freezer is a mess."

"I'll clean up, Linda." Daniel sponged and wiped while his sister sat on the fruit crate and wept.

"Why do we have to live like this?" Linda sobbed. "No lights, no refrigerator, nothing! How can you live like this, Mamma? Mrs. Henderson has a frost-free refrigerator. Her freezer never makes a mess."

"Oh, Linda." Mamma stroked the girl's hair. She looked troubled.

"Why must we be so poor, Mamma?"

"Things could be worse, Linda." Mamma soothed the girl. "We must thank God for the good things He gives us and not complain when we cannot afford everything other people have."

"Oh, Mamma, how can you live like this? Mrs. Henderson has an iron, a dryer, a vacuum cleaner, a television, everything! When we have money, Mamma, you must buy the things Mrs. Henderson has. They will make you happy."

"Oh, Linda! Things do not make a person happy. It is people who make each other happy."

Daniel was through cleaning the stale-smelling refrigerator. He felt annoyed with Linda. His sister had changed. The life she saw at the Hendersons' was spoiling her. She was getting dissatisfied and wanted all the things she saw at the Anglo house.

"We will get along without electricity," Daniel told Linda. "Main thing is we can

36

cook, for there is gas left in the butane tank.''

In his windowless room, Daniel was not so sure he could do without lights. Even with the door open, he had to grope for his things. He'd keep the five-dollar bill, he resolved. The family needed money more badly than Sarge did.

Monday morning, Daniel overslept and so did Linda. Drizzling fog had pushed in from the ocean overnight. They breakfasted in a hurry and started walking to town. Linda wore Mamma's black shawl over her smooth hair. Daniel walked bareheaded. Thick vapor clouds drifted over the road along the reservoir, giving everything an eerie feeling.

''I am scared,'' said Linda, grasping Daniel's hand.

''It's only fog, Linda.'' Daniel did not admit to his own weird feeling. They stayed on the road. Linda clutched her brother's hand.

''I hear something.''

The two stopped and listened. Faint voices quavered near the road. Daniel stooped, trying to penetrate the fog. Glasses were useless in this kind of weather; he had left them at home.

A small creature wobbled to his feet. Daniel lifted the shivering body. It was a kitten. Daniel tucked the wet creature into his sweatshirt. ''Poor kitty. Somebody got rid of you,'' he muttered.

''She will make you dirty,'' Linda warned.

37

"She will die if nobody saves her," Daniel replied.

"She will scratch you," Linda persisted.

"Scratches heal." Daniel stopped. "I hear another kitten across the road."

"Let somebody else save the cats. We're going to be late, Daniel."

"It won't take long." Daniel hunted up the second stray. His calls brought three more kittens to his feet. Littermates? Daniel tucked the furry lot under his sweatshirt. Instead of purring, the kittens cried and got away. Daniel stooped again and again, picking up cats. His arms overflowed with the colorful lot. The kittens wouldn't stay in place, though.

"Go ahead," Daniel called in a frenzy. "I must save these cats."

Linda cried, "I am scared, Daniel. This is a bad road and the fog makes it worse."

"So help me carry these cats," Daniel suggested. "They need warm milk and a home."

"But Mrs. Henderson . . ."

"Can't you think of anything but that woman?" Daniel blurted. "She is warm and dry. These kitties are freezing."

"I am going by myself," Linda howled. "It's your fault if anything happens to me."

Daniel felt like crying. The kittens scratched and scrambled. He hastened downhill, losing two of them. At the village, three remained under his sweatshirt.

Light shone from the postal trailer. Daniel climbed the steps and let himself in. The postal clerk stood behind the counter. She looked at the cats with big, round eyes. "What's with these cats?" she screeched.

"They need a home," Daniel said bravely. "Can I leave them with you? People come in for mail. They'll give them a home."

"I don't want them in here!" The clerk threw up her arms. "Take these cats out of here. They do not belong in a post office." She picked up a ruler and started after him. Daniel scrambled outside, almost stumbling over a kitten he dropped.

What to do with the strays? Down the street Daniel caught his breath. He quietly opened Mr. Randall's gate and let himself in. He found an old rag and dried the kittens' fur. Mr. Randall's empty doghouse made a cozy shelter. He backtracked, found the stray under the trailer steps, and put it with the other orphans.

Humming, Daniel dashed up to the Hendersons' house. The poodle yipped and his sister came out. "What do you want?"

"A bowl of warm milk," Daniel pleaded.

Linda looked sullen. "Mrs. Henderson was late for work. She said if I cannot come on time, she will take Junior to the nursery and I can sleep all day. She was *angry,* Daniel."

"I am sorry," Daniel stuttered. He had forgotten about Linda's problem.

Linda cheered up. "Mrs. Henderson said she'll buy me an alarm clock I can take home Friday. Then I won't ever wake up late again."

Daniel grinned. "How about milk for the kittens?"

"How many are you feeding?"

"Three. I lost two in the fog." Daniel waited outside until Linda brought the milk.

"Is this enough?" she asked.

"*Sí, hermana, gracias.*" Daniel spoke Spanish, he was so happy.

At Mr. Randall's, Daniel nudged the kittens to the bowl. They lapped up the milk. Before long, the bowl was empty. Daniel put the kittens into the doghouse and waited until they purred. He rushed back uphill, hoping to find the strays.

Near the dam, Daniel called into the fog. He strained to hear mewing voices. Suddenly a car lurched into the turnout. Who would park there on a bleak morning like this, Daniel wondered? Music from the radio blared through an open car window. The motor died. Doors slammed, and footsteps crunched on the gravel.

chapter five

Why Do Things Change?

Squinting, Daniel recognized the outlines of three men. All carried sticklike objects. The men kicked at discarded cans as they walked to the gate. They slipped through the turnstile and soon their footsteps thudded on the dam.

Before the men vanished in the fog, a pickup truck crunched up the road. It parked beside the car. Its lights went out, but the driver stayed inside the cab. Daniel's heart pounded. He wished he had brought his glasses. Something strange was going on. Across the reservoir, cattle bellowed and stampeded. Shots rang out. Then there was silence.

After a while, men's subdued voices became audible on the dam. Daniel heard footsteps, huffing and puffing, and the sounds of a heavy body being dragged over gravel. Had the rancher shot a cow? Three men dragged a large animal through the gate and hoisted the carcass up into the truck. The tailgate clanked and the pickup truck roared off. The men hopped into their car and followed the pickup. Blood pounded in Daniel's ears. The rancher lived in the opposite direction!

Daniel abandoned the hunt for the kittens. He hastened out into the valley and asked for work. He mowed a few lawns and picked up things at the store that he knew Mamma needed.

In New Almaden, Daniel listened at Mr. Randall's gate. No sound came from the doghouse. Daniel guessed his elderly friend had been feeding the kittens. He hurried uphill, hoping he'd spot the other strays somewhere.

"Imagine, somebody dumped those cats on the road," Daniel told Mamma at home. He did not tell her about the cattle rustlers, about Linda's being late for work, or about the five dollars he kept in his pocket. Mamma mustn't get upset.

Next day's hunt for the kittens turned up nothing. Wednesday morning, the sun came out bright and clean. "Today I will harvest tea," Daniel told Mamma.

"Take the baby with you, Daniel. She always runs after you when you leave."

"*Sí,* Mamma." Daniel bounced his delighted sister all the way to Reservoir Road. "Now you must walk," he told her. The child's legs were straighter than they used to be. Angelina no longer waddled like a duck. She grasped the end of his stick and made a giggly game of pulling at it.

Dainty blossoms covered the bank which tilted toward the morning sun. Daniel clambered down, carrying Angelina. As he threaded his way over the sunbaked ground, Daniel marvelled how such fragrant plants could thrive in this hard soil. Each plant covered ground. Massed together, the plants shielded the soil from erosion. Daniel picked the blossoms, careful not to pull out the roots.

Some plants had shed their petals, leaving yellow pompons to go to seed. Daniel left them alone. His sacks filled quickly. The bank grew enough tea for a whole town to quit the coffee habit. Daniel chuckled. He did not care for coffee.

After the sacks were filled, Daniel followed the trail along the creek. Different plants had sprouted in the mud and started to cover the soil left exposed by the receding water. Nature was healing itself, Daniel observed. God had arranged things well; only people kept ruining things. Daniel remembered a day when he had looked for his favorite berry bushes only to find that a bulldozer had ripped them out.

A car passed on the road. The silver-haired driver and the woman beside him waved. Daniel waved back, wondering why older Anglo people lived apart from younger folk. In many migrant families, the members of the different generations lived together until death. Daniel suddenly missed the relatives, especially Granny Rosita. Poor Rosita, no doubt she was missing her husband in her now-so-silent world! Tears welled up in Daniel's eyes.

"Why do things have to change?" he muttered. "Why can't the family be together?" Daniel wished he knew how to put his faith in the Lord, like Alfredo did on his deathbed.

Migrants worked until they could no longer stoop in the field. The relatives had spoken of diabetes, high blood pressure, asthma, and stroke. Migrants lived shorter lives than Anglos. They often died in middle age. Anglo people were healthier because they visited doctors more often, Daniel reasoned.

Daniel put the sacks of tea in a shady spot. The voice of a bullfrog beckoned. The frog lay somewhere below the rippling branches of a cottonwood tree.

In the half-submerged grasses along the shore, Daniel saw not one, but five bullfrogs. Four splashed into the water. The fifth frog stayed in the patchy sunlight, too comfortable to move. Daniel chuckled.

Fish snapped, making growing circles. Two white birds soared, wheeled, and plunged. Fantastic fishermen, they got their catch feet first. Angelina clapped her hands and Daniel stood spellbound.

Watching the large birds, Daniel paid little attention to the men in blue jeans. They were coming down the road in pairs. Each man carried a stick and a litter bag. Angelina saw them and screamed. Daniel picked her up.

"Nobody's going to hurt you, Baby."

The blue-jeaned men fanned out along the road and picked up discards. Broken bottles, shotgun shells, beer cans, and paper scraps went into the litter bags.

Black men, Chicanos, and Anglos passed Daniel. Angelina scratched and scrambled like a frightened kitten. Daniel asked God to heal his little sister from her fear of people.

The blue-jeaned men returned to the dam and put the litter bags beside the garbage cans. A big man waited for them in a panel truck. The men filed into the truck and were driven downhill. Daniel turned back to get his bags of tea. The roadside was cleaner than he appreciated, for the blue-jeaned men had also picked up his tea.

When Daniel told Mamma what had happened, she gave him a strange look. "Did you really pick tea, Daniel? Are you telling the truth?"

"*Sí*, Mamma."

"You are the man of the family," she reminded Daniel. "Are you doing your job?"

Daniel gulped. He resolved to bring home money soon, so she'd know he was *trying*.

Daniel spent Wednesday afternoon harvesting tea and spreading blossoms on papers in the yard. Mamma said she'd supervise the drying.

Thursday, Daniel left home early. While walking, he saw the white birds again. They plunged, feet first, after fish. Daniel had forgotten to check his bird book.

Daniel did not slow his pace until nearing New Almaden. The white mare stood in the corral, looking sleepy. A tiny foal lay behind her. Its brown coat was clean, though the foal rested in the turf. A rooster strutted about the mare, thrusting out arched tail feathers. Red comb high, he crowed, as though announcing glad tidings: A new life has begun!

The foal sported a blaze. Its reddish eyelashes and silky hairs glistened in the morning sun. His mother stood watch beside him. She was soiled and stood in the wet spot where the birth had occurred. For days, she had appeared sluggish and didn't pay attention to anything. She had been heavy with foal and now the baby had arrived.

The foal stretched in the sunshine. Its tail flicked over its pudgy rump. Daniel felt glad to be alive. The young horse brought out feelings of tenderness in Daniel. He had felt this way when Angelina was a baby. Helpless, she cried for him to pick her up. She used to kick her tiny feet at him, waiting to be lifted, stopping her crying the moment he picked her up.

Daniel's face felt hot, thinking of Angelina, the baby who had spent so much time at the edge of a field. Sometimes he'd fashioned a sunshade for her, and sometimes he covered her with his jacket to keep out wind and rain. Daniel had not thought of these things for a long time.

Linda also grew up in the fields. For once, Daniel did not feel bitter about Linda's not wanting to follow the crops. For once, he did not blame her for spurning the migrant life. For once, he did not frown at Linda's desiring a bed for the babies she'd have some day. Linda was a girl. To girls such things made a difference, Daniel guessed.

In the village, Daniel checked on the kittens. All three huddled together in the doghouse, making a furry bundle. Mr. Randall had been feeding them, Daniel knew.

Daniel marched out into the valley, passing the suburbs this time. At an intersection he entered a shopping center. A sign caught his eye: *Herb Teas*. He waited until the store opened. The black-haired clerk smiled at him. "Do you want something?" she asked.

Daniel fumbled in his pocket and produced wilted blossoms. "My mother says this is a good tea," he explained.

The clerk sniffed and nodded. "It's chamomile, smells fresh."

"I could harvest some for you," Daniel offered.

"Oh, really? How much do you charge?"

"I will take groceries, if you have any," Daniel replied without thinking.

"It's a deal. Bring the tea when it's good and dry."

"Yes, ma'am." Daniel praised his good fortune. Leaving the health-food store behind, he went into stores and offered his services. Nobody hired a youngster, Daniel found out. He did not understand why. Even little children worked in fields and orchards, earning money for their families. In the city, nobody trusted a child to do adult labor.

The long, hot walk left Daniel tired. He turned homeward. In New Almaden, he did not even knock on Mr. Randall's door. Before climbing Reservoir Road, he rested on the bridge banister. It was then he glanced at the church and gasped. The beautiful eucalyptus trees stood beheaded. Without leaves, branches, or boughs, they looked like unhappy giants. Daniel fled the bridge.

At home, Daniel went straight for the faucet. No water came out! He jiggled the faucet.

"No use trying, Daniel. The man from the water company was out and cut us off." Mamma looked upset.

"Didn't you pay him?"

"No, Daniel. The landlord took Linda's eight dollars. It was all we had."

"Couldn't the landlord wait till next week?"

"No. He said he will turn us out if we don't pay him soon. Where will we live without this wonderful cabin, Daniel? The landlord will be back!"

Daniel filled the bucket, scooping water from the creek. He felt like a failure. Papa always had managed to pay for water and electricity. Now, that he, Daniel, was man of the family there was lack in everything.

"I must learn how to have faith," Daniel told himself. "I must learn to pray." He picked up the bucket and carried it up to the cabin.

"Here is water, Mamma. Cheer up!" Daniel put the bucket into the sink.

"The landlord, Daniel. Where will we go if he turns us out?" Mamma wept softly. Daniel fingered his pocket. He cleared his throat.

"I, uh, made some money today. The woman at the health-food store sent me on errands." He produced the sergeant's five-dollar bill. It had rested in his pocket all along.

"*Es verdad,* Daniel?"

"*Si,* Mamma."

Daniel laid the money on the table. He hated to lie, but Mamma's crying stabbed at his heart.

At dawn, Daniel left quietly, so as not to disturb Mamma and Angelina. He headed for the tea field. Commuters passed him, Air Force people, student drivers, and also a highway patrol car.

Daniel worked at his tea harvest, enjoying the morning breeze. Suddenly, a car came to an abrupt halt above the spot where Daniel worked.

chapter SIX

Mamma Needs Medicine

Daniel looked up. Sarge leaned out of the car. "Have you seen a little brown package anywhere—like the one you kept for me?"

"Where should I have seen it?" Daniel asked.

"In the weeds, or over the shoulder somewhere. That fool Leonard threw it out."

"I haven't seen it. What's in it anyway?"

"None of your business," Sarge blurted. He calmed down. "Tell you what, kid. I'll give you another five dollars if you look around and find it for me."

Daniel felt confused. Why was Sarge so angry when the content of the package was mentioned? And why had Leonard thrown the package out of the car?

"By the way," Sarge asked. "What did you do with the five I gave you?"

"I, uh, gave it to my mother," Daniel stuttered.

"Then you better keep your mouth shut about the money, or the package, if somebody asks you. And don't you tell the police you know me, or they'll lock you in!''

The car roared off. Daniel swallowed hard. What mess had he gotten himself into? While he filled his bags, he kept fighting his rising fear.

The rattle of Linda's new alarm clock jolted Daniel out of bed Monday morning. His feet hit the floor. They mustn't be late again.

Linda was up, heating beans and tea. She was in a bad mood. The landlord had taken her eight dollars and Daniel's five. To worsen matters, she brought home only change last Friday. Mrs. Henderson deducted the price of the alarm clock from the girl's pay.

"No light, no water, nothing," Linda grumbled. "How can Mamma live like this?"

Linda's bad mood rankled Daniel. "Food tastes just as good in the dark and creek water is as good as faucet water," he stressed. They ate in the light of hissing gas flames, then carried the dishes to the sink. Daniel headed for the door. "Are you ready?"

"Uh-huh."

Clouds covered the sky. Night hawks circled, dove, and banked. They fed on insects. Daniel watched the birds. Some flew so low he could see the white bars on their wings.

Muddy tracks showed where a car had been dragged over the bank the day before, and flares littered the road.

Linda passed the flares and tracks without comment. In the canyon, her nose wrinkled. "What's that?" she asked. Daniel sniffed. Bad odors rose from the roadside. Linda frowned. "Maybe your kittens died."

"I hope not."

"The change was too much for them, Daniel. Pets can't handle life in the wild."

Daniel sighed. He did not feel like talking about change. Too many changes had taken place.

At the Hendersons', Linda handed her brother old newspapers and plastic sacks. Daniel harvested tea on his way home. Mamma helped him spread the blossoms. She was breathing hard. Daniel knelt beside her.

"How long until I can take the tea to the store?" Daniel asked. He repeated his question. What was wrong? Why was it Mamma did not answer? He looked over his shoulder. Her ashen face scared him.

"Are you all right?"

"*Sí,* Daniel. Do not worry about me." Mamma's breath whistled. Daniel took her into the house. What was the matter with Mamma? Something was wrong. She had been getting upset lately and sometimes she even cried.

Next morning, Mamma sat in bed, eyes

bulging. "My pills, Daniel! Get me my pill!"

Daniel ran to the refrigerator, where Mamma kept her medicine. He twisted the bottle, ready to catch the tiny white pill. The cap came off. No pill fell out. Daniel peered into the bottle. It was empty.

Ever since Mamma's surgery, she had taken these pills. Now they had no money to fill the bottle. How long had she been without medicine? Daniel plodded into the bedroom, desperately asking God to help keep Mamma safe.

"I will get medicine for you. I'll be back soon, Mamma."

"We have no money," she fretted.

"I know, Mamma. I will bring medicine, don't worry." Daniel fetched extra pillows and propped her up. "Can you breathe better with these?"

"*Sí*, Daniel, *gracias*."

"I will take Angelina, so she won't bother you." Daniel pulled a dress over his sister.

On the road, Daniel did some thinking. Mamma needed the cabin. It was a shelter where she could rest. Following the crops, she might not find a single cool resting place in California's hot valleys.

Poor Mamma, she had worked hard in the fields. Now she could no longer stand the heat. Daniel kept swallowing the lump that pushed up into his throat.

If only Papa could rush home! Papa was a grown man and knew what to do. Daniel talked to God. But God was far away and there was no telling where Papa was.

If only Papa could write! He and Uncle Felix had attended school sometimes, between field work. They hadn't learned much, though. If Papa and his brother wanted to send a letter, they had to find somebody who could write.

Daniel felt lucky he had attended school a whole year while the family lived in New Almaden. The schoolbus had picked him up and the teacher was nice. But there was so much more to learn!

Like where to get medicine for Mamma.

Daniel lifted Angelina in his arms. He hurried downhill, hoping Linda would know something.

At the town's entrance, people clustered together. An artist sat by the church, sketchbook propped up on his knees. Daniel peeked over the artist's shoulder. The church made a pretty picture, what with the pointed windows, turrets, and steep roof.

The artist shifted his folding chair and sketched the church from a different angle. He paid little attention to onlookers. A woman stopped her car beside Daniel.

"Is this the church where they're supposed to shoot the wedding scene?" the woman asked.

Daniel held the kicking Angelina. "I don't know."

The woman pointed to her watch.

"They're supposed to be here now. It was in the paper." She parked beside the creek and waited.

Daniel climbed to the Henderson house. The poodle yipped and Linda peeked through the window. She ran outside and hoisted Angelina in her arms. Eyes flashing, she asked, "Have you seen the movie people, Daniel? They're supposed to shoot a wedding scene by the church."

"An artist is sitting by the church and people are waiting." Daniel did not feel like making small talk. "Mamma needs medicine, Linda. Can you get some money?"

"You mean ahead of time?" Linda frowned.

"*Sí.*"

"Mrs. Henderson keeps no money in the house, Daniel. She gets her paycheck Friday and cashes it at the bank."

"Do we have credit somewhere—at the drugstore maybe?" Daniel asked, even though he knew better.

"No, Daniel. Who would give us credit?" Linda's face grew long.

"Where did Papa buy the medicine? Do you know?"

"It's on the bottle. Did you bring it?"

"*Sí.*" Daniel pulled the empty pill bottle out of his jeans pocket. Reading the label, he recognized the pharmacy's address. What made Linda so smart, he wondered?

Linda put Angelina down. The Henderson toddler was screaming in the house. "I hope you get Mamma's medicine," Linda told her brother. "I must see what's wrong with Junior; he's getting into everything."

"Can't you keep Angelina for me?"

"Not today, Daniel. Mrs. Henderson is having a baby shower for a woman she works with. There'll be lots of women in the house. It's going to be a party. I must wash windows, vacuum, iron, wax the kitchen, clean the bathroom . . ."

"I get the message, Linda. Angelina will be underfoot."

"I am sorry, Daniel, but I am *working*."

"I understand." Daniel remembered that Sarge had promised him five dollars for finding the lost package. Perhaps he'd find the thing. Five dollars would pay for medicine, he hoped.

Daniel hoisted his little sister onto his shoulders and entered a shortcut along the summer-dry canal. The people in charge of the water district had covered the service road with crushed rock. It was hard to walk on. The rock was red; it held much cinnabar. Indians of old came from all over the West to get the vermilion color. They crushed the ore and painted their bodies with the toxic mercury powder. "Inviting skin cancer," the teacher had explained at school. Daniel kept clear of the stuff.

Branches snapped. A deer broke through the brush. It was alarmed perhaps by the roar of vehicles which passed through the village below. At the end of the service road, Daniel climbed a winding trail to a stand of laurels and live oaks.

"Hush, Angelina," Daniel whispered. He felt spooky, for they had entered a strange world. A hum and rustle sounded everywhere. Angelina clung to her brother. Gnarled boughs lay across the path, leaning into each other's arms like giant brothers. Rushing winter rains had gouged out king-sized roots. A squirrel coughed overhead and kept it up.

"Hush, Angelina," Daniel repeated. He lifted his chin to high tree crowns, wondering if something might pounce on them. A dry creekbed, strewn with rocks, led them to trail's end, where the green dimness yielded to yellow sunlight.

Fences showed, then a water tank, and a cottage between dusty shrubs. Daniel hastened past the place, praying nobody would chase them off. Angelina must not hear harsh words. She was such a frightened child.

Much to Daniel's surprise, the path came out on Reservoir Road. Only, the road looked different.

All manner of vehicles stood along the road. Signs closed the road to through traffic. People milled about the bridge, carrying all sorts of props. Daniel dallied on the bridge.

A burly man stood in the creek below, giving directions. Wiry fellows adjusted a glaring panel, while a tall man eased down a box on a cable. Two men held up a large spotlight.

"Look for your shadow!" the burly man shouted. "Look for sunspots behind you!"

The wiry fellows wrestled with the panel. Beside them, a cameraman struggled for footing. On a blanket beside the rushing creek sat a grown girl. She let an older woman slip a blonde wig over her head, stood up, and arranged her long gown and the large wool shawl over her shoulders.

The older woman put a doll at the water's edge and stepped back. The girl entered the creek. Her "ooh" told Daniel the water was cold. She ducked, fell backward, and went under. Coming up, she lay in the water, the long blonde hair covering her face. Daniel grew frantic.

"Help! Somebody help her!"

Instead of helping the motionless girl, the burly man scowled up at the bridge. "What's going on up there? Who's that smart aleck?"

People shouted from all directions. They scowled at the boy as if he had committed a terrible crime. The tall man who had lowered the box approached Daniel.

"You're not supposed to be here," the man said. "We are shooting a movie and you mustn't interfere."

"I, uh, didn't know." Daniel felt miserable. He guessed the tall man was important, for his nametag read "Assistant Director."

The blonde girl in the water coughed. The older woman adjusted the doll and stepped back again. The girl slipped, fell backward. She floated, the hair covering her face. Daniel clamped his mouth shut. She really looked dead. The burly man's voice sounded above the creek.

"Action!"

"Hold it!"

"Cut!"

"Take that young lady to a hot shower."

The girl left the water. She shed the dripping wig, shawl, and skirt. She was wearing a wet suit. Somebody assisted her up the bank. Her face was blue and her teeth chattered. The assistant director took her to one of the trailers.

The older woman now put the doll into the water. She tilted the doll's head and twisted the waxlike arm. The current swept the doll downstream. Somebody retrieved the doll and gave it back to the woman. She tied a string around the doll's neck and fastened the string to a rock. She adjusted the doll's head and arm and stepped back. The burly man bellowed.

"We can't use her. She's a mask. We need an expression of fright. Nobody will believe that doll is scared. It doesn't look right."

Angelina started to scream. Daniel no longer could keep her quiet. He fled from the bridge.

The tall man called Daniel back. "Don't run off, boy! Come back!"

chapter seven

Spotlight on Angelina

Daniel returned to the bridge, struggling to keep his little sister in his arms. "Yes, sir?"

"Let me see her face," the assistant director ordered. "Turn her around, so I can see her face."

"She's afraid of strangers," Daniel explained, lifting Angelina's tear-stained face.

"She's perfect," the assistant director decided. He called down to the burly man. "Listen, we've got the perfect child."

"Where?" The burly man glanced up at Angelina. "Why, she's a Mexican. We need a fair type."

"We can always change the script," the tall man suggested. "An exotic child can add drama to the plot."

"O.K., bring her down."

The tall man reached for Angelina. Daniel clutched his sister. The tall man chuckled. "Nothing will happen to her. We'll ask your father's permission if you want."

"You can't, sir. Papa is out of town."

"What about your mother?"

"She lives in Twin Creek up the road. But

you mustn't bother her. She's sick right now.''

"Listen," the tall man decided. "We'll give you fifty dollars if you let us use the child for one short scene. We're in a terrible rush. We must shoot two more scenes in this area before the sun goes down.''

"Money?" Daniel asked.

"Money.''

Daniel sucked in his breath. He thought of Mamma, wheezing in the big bed, getting sicker without medicine. How would Papa decide? Would Papa give the child to strangers? Daniel wished he did not have to make such a big decision. Mamma needed help, though. She was in bad shape and getting worse.

Daniel handed the girl to the assistant director. "Be gentle with her. She's awfully scared.''

Somebody hustled the bristling child down to the water. The older woman put Angelina on the blanket, and the burly man gave directions. The spotlight shone on Daniel's sister and cameras clicked.

Angelina sat like a cornered animal. Strangers stood around her and a man with a camera moved in for a close-up. Angelina suddenly backed up. Her scream rent the air as she fell over a rock. Her head tilted. One brown arm drifting, she was swept up by the current.

"Help, somebody help her!" Daniel

stumbled down to the creek. By the time he reached the water, somebody had fished Angelina out. Daniel took the girl into his arms. He was crying almost as loudly as the dripping child was.

"Go 'way!" Daniel fought off everybody who came in his way.

The tall man caught Daniel on the bridge and led him to one of the trailers. A golden star was pasted on the door.

The girl who had "drowned" earlier stood there. Smiling, she reached for Angelina. "Give me the babe," she said softly.

Daniel let go of his sister. The older woman brought dry clothes. She put them inside the trailer in exchange for Angelina's wet clothes. She put the soggy bundle beside Daniel.

The assistant director came back. "Here's your money. Don't lose it."

"I won't." Daniel fumbled with the crisp bill. It showed the number 50 in the corners.

"Aren't you going to say 'thank you'?" the tall man asked.

"You hurt my sister!" Daniel blurted.

The tall man laughed. "She's all right. So she got wet, 'twas no worse than slipping in the bathtub."

The girl who had "drowned" earlier brought Daniel's little sister outside. Daniel gulped.

Angelina looked like a doll stuck in an old-fashioned, too-big dress. Her tiny face almost disappeared between puffed-up sleeves. The sash went twice around her waist, and the skirt swept the ground. Worst, her hair looked like a rat's nest.

"Are you O.K., Baby?" Daniel asked. Angelina did not smile and she did not giggle. No sound came out of her. Daniel rushed her past the parked vehicles. On the way, he wrestled with her hair. It was no use. Only Mamma and Linda knew how to straighten Angelina's hair. In his distress, Daniel carried her up to Linda.

"Please do not make a fuss, Linda. Can you fix the baby's hair and dry her clothes? Mamma mustn't see her like this. She's sick already."

"What happened to her?" Linda appeared shocked.

"Angelina acted in the movie and we got fifty dollars. See?" Daniel showed the bill. "If you make the baby look like herself again I'll tell you all about it. Right now, Mamma needs her medicine."

"All right, Daniel."

Daniel hurried to the shopping center. He found the pharmacy and got the pills. On the way home, he picked up Angelina. Her clothes felt dryer-warm. Her hair was neatly tied with a ribbon. Daniel felt grateful. Linda was a helpful girl, after all.

But Angelina did not giggle once. At

home, she crawled into bed beside Mamma and hid under the cover.

Mamma slumped in bed. She was coughing. Daniel gave her the pill and she washed it down with water. *"Gracias,"* she whispered.

Daniel opened the window. A fresh breeze rushed in. Mamma gulped and breathed easier. Daniel plumped her pillows. He felt so sorry for his mother that he hurt. She had fought a tough battle, but now the pill was working. She was falling asleep and Angelina was sleeping too.

The boy tiptoed out of the house. Linda had lost time fussing over Angelina. He must help her. He jogged down to New Almaden and pushed the vacuum cleaner at the Henderson house. It was the least he could do.

When Daniel returned home, Mamma was awake. She smiled. "The pill helped me, Daniel. *Muchas gracias.*"

"It was nothing, Mamma. Are you hungry?"

"Sí, Daniel. Did you put beans on the stove?"

Daniel felt stupid. He could have bought food, for he had much money in his pocket. He was glad Mamma forgot to ask him how he got the medicine. After bad spells, she seemed to remember nothing.

Next morning, Mamma asked Daniel, "Why is Angelina so strange? She doesn't want to get out of bed."

"She's tired, Mamma. She did much walking yesterday."

"What else did she do, Daniel?"

"We were very lucky, Mamma." Daniel forced a grin. "Movie people shot pictures by the bridge. They took Angelina's picture and gave me money for it."

"Are you speaking the truth, Daniel?"

"*Si*, Mamma. Ask Linda."

"What did Linda have to do with it?" Mamma's searching look made Daniel's cheeks burn.

"She, uh, combed Angelina's hair."

"Did Linda leave the Henderson house?"

"No, Mamma. I took the baby up to her."

"How much money did the movie people give you?"

"Fifty dollars. Look!" Daniel put the bills and change on the table. "This much is left over after the medicine."

"It's too much, Daniel. Give it back."

"The movie people were glad they got Angelina's picture, Mamma. We need the money for the landlord."

Tears glistened on Mamma's face. "I know you speak the truth, Daniel. You never lied to me before."

"Tell me what we need from the store, Mamma. Today we can buy anything we want."

"We must not waste the money, Daniel. Get beans and flour. Maybe the lady at the health-food store will give you rice when the tea is dry.''

''*Sí*, Mamma.'' Daniel marched off, got the food, and lugged two sacks up Reservoir Road.

The forenoon was sunny, but a yellow truck crawled up the road, lights on high beam. A chute rose from the truck, spraying evil-smelling chemicals at the trees and shrubs.

Daniel let the sacks slide from his shoulders. Wherever he had walked, the sprayed trees had more bugs than those that never got any spray. Spraying killed the good bugs with the bad. Even the teacher said so. She once told the class in her crisp English, ''Insects develop resistance and revenge themselves with an increased reproduction rate. With the predators killed off, the prey animals multiply unchecked.''

Daniel loathed spraying. In the valleys where migrants worked, crop dusters flew low, spraying chemicals that made everybody sick. He did not feel like walking behind deadly fumes, for already he was coughing. He hoisted the sacks, crossed over, and got ahead of the truck.

At home, Daniel put the sacks into the family's fruit-crate cupboards. Mamma was smiling through the open door. She was resting in bed.

''Are you still doing your exercise,

Mamma? Have you been walking?'' Daniel inquired.

"*Si,* Daniel. Every morning I walk in the shade, like the doctor ordered.''

"When the weather cools off in the fall, we can walk together,'' Daniel ventured. "Then you can see the beautiful lake and the birds I've been telling you about.''

"*Si,* Daniel. And maybe we can go to the church again.'' Mamma looked wistful. They had been worshiping on their own. On weekends, when Linda was home, Mamma would tell them religious stories. Then they'd kneel and ask God to help keep the relatives safe. Mamma always spoke a special prayer for Granny Rosita, and they all said "Amen.''

Daniel noticed the red sandals beside Mamma's bed. The sandals were Rosita's special present to Mamma, and she loved to wear them. Daniel sighed.

"Why do things have to change, Mamma? Why did Alfredo have to die? Why must we be without Papa?''

Mamma looked surprised. "And who promised that life should be a bed of roses, Daniel? Did not our Lord Jesus wear a crown of thorns? Did He not carry a cross up that Golgotha hill? He was the Son of God, Daniel. We are only migrants. Why should we have it better?''

"But, Mamma,'' Daniel interrupted.

"Our Lord Jesus is now in heaven in all His glory."

"And we will get our reward also," Mamma intoned. "Our Lord Jesus said, 'Rejoice and be glad, for your reward is great.' "

Mamma always found words to comfort her family. Daniel wished he could be like Mamma, so full of faith and hope. He did not want her to know that sometimes he got angry, and sometimes he got depressed. She had her own cross to carry, what with that manmade valve clicking inside her chest.

Daniel hated to leave Mamma, but she sent him away to check on his tea. Angelina stayed. He could not coax her out of bed.

Chemical fumes hung over the plants. Daniel felt like crying. The tea was ruined.

The people from the water district had drained water from the reservoir to swell the creek for the movie people. A great mud flat shimmered around a few tall skeleton trees. While debating what to do, Daniel noticed one of the large white birds he had seen earlier. He still had not looked in his bird book.

The bird winged across the road. On the hillside, it lighted on the bare branch of an oak.

Daniel ran to the pasture fence. He must see that bird close up, so that he could identify it. He slipped through the wire. Tall grasses, rocks, and squirrel holes slowed his climb.

Looking back, Daniel saw the reservoir below. It glimmered and danced in the morning breeze. He had scaled the hill, but the white bird flew higher. The hill was only the first rise in a series of hills. Daniel followed the bird.

chapter eight

Man in the Mud

Twigs and leaves rustled underfoot as Daniel climbed higher. He entered a trail where deer and cattle tracks showed. Steep hills overgrown with shrubs loomed ahead. But where was the white bird?

Daniel rested, catching his breath. Branches blocked his view. He could not see the reservoir. He turned back, for not a trace of the large bird showed anywhere.

On the descent, something glistened near a fresh mound of brown soil. Daniel adjusted his glasses. A plastic strip stuck out of the hump's sunlit side. It was longer than his hand and two fingers wide. One edge was smooth, the other edge punctured with holes. Daniel poked into the dirt. He hit metal.

A prickly sensation crept over Daniel's back. Was somebody watching him? Glancing over his shoulder, he saw—nobody. He dug up a small tin can and pried off the lid.

A plastic sack inside contained white crystals. As he was about to taste the stuff,

Daniel remembered the sheriff who had looked for narcotics.

Daniel lifted the sack. As he was ready to scatter the crystals, he saw the animal tracks. He wouldn't want to harm deer or cattle. Daniel retied the sack, closed the lid, and reburied the can. The marker he flung into the poison oak rambling over the hillside.

Shots suddenly banged against canyon walls. Daniel ducked. Were the shots a warning?

"Dear God," Daniel gasped. "Please don't let them hit me, for who would look after Mamma? Who would take Linda to work?"

Daniel hastened from the spot and swung left. A boulder-strewn oak grove led down to a draw. In the broken shade of the oaks, he dashed from boulder to boulder, dodging possible bullets.

Daniel reached a corral fence and pulled himself up behind a cattle trough. The draw bristled with water holes. Swamp grasses and fat yellow flowers nodded on watery islands. Daniel backtracked through the cool water. Above the spring, he found himself out in the open.

On the road below, a car careened around the bend. Men shouted something in passing. The shooting stopped. A car started up and speeded down the road. Relief washed over

Daniel. He was safe! He reached the road, which seemed peaceful enough. Birds twittered and an airplane hummed a drowsy tune overhead.

It was then he saw the sign at the gate:

No Trespassing!
Violators Will Be Punished by Law!

Daniel gulped. He had broken the law!

Ahead of Daniel, the blue-jeaned men fanned out over the road. Along turnouts and curves, they picked up beer cans, bottles, and other litter.

Daniel guessed the men's backs were hurting, even as Papa's back was hurting now, somewhere in a hot field. The blue-jeaned men came every Wednesday. The large man always stayed in the panel truck. He wore a sport shirt and regular slacks, not jeans. Was he a labor boss, Daniel wondered? Somebody who hired, maybe? Daniel approached the panel truck. The large man spoke to him first.

"Young fellow, you better not hang around here while my men are cleaning up," he advised, sounding friendly.

"Did you hire them?" Daniel inquired.

The man chuckled. "These men have hired themselves, young fellow. They stole and drank and speeded themselves right into county jail."

"Jail!" Shivers ran through Daniel. Two young Chicanos trudged up from the reservoir. They put neatly-tied litter bags beside the garbage cans.

Rattled, Daniel ran downhill. At the corral, he did not even feel like stopping by the mare and her colt.

Trucks with heavy loads pulled uphill and Daniel watched his step on the shoulder. The trucks carried gravel for road surfacing. Daniel guessed there was construction work to be done on the side road leading to the Air Force base. He wondered if a kid might get a job there.

At the church, Daniel noticed that a side door stood open. Piles of scrap lumber and heaps of broken pots lay about. It was unlike the persons in charge of the church to leave that door open, Daniel reflected.

In town, Mr. Randall waved at Daniel from his yard. He was watching two kittens at play. Daniel looked about for the third kitten. Mr. Randall laughed.

"I found a home for it, Daniel. These two kitties I'll keep. They're my favorites."

"You are a kind man, Mr. Randall." Daniel felt like hugging his white-haired friend. Mr. Randall had been in poor health lately. Daniel wished he knew words to soothe his friend, words of faith and hope, like Mamma spoke to the family. Instead, he talked about what was bothering him.

"Why do things change, Mr. Randall? Why can't things stay the same once they are good?"

Mr. Randall's faded blue eyes looked kind. "There have been plenty of changes in my life, Daniel. Changes are like storms that rip leaves from the trees, like snow that covers new plants. Every change is a challenge, Daniel. Without change, we'd have no seasons and no new growth."

Daniel sighed. He'd mull over the long speech later. For now he said, "I must find work today, so Mamma knows I am trying to help. I am the man of the family, you know."

"Why not ask the owner of the house down the street if he can use you," Mr. Randall suggested. "He's building an addition to his house. Tell him I sent you."

"Verdad?"

Daniel ran past the town's quaint cottages and Casa Grande, the old mansion left from the town's quicksilver mining days. New Almadeners were taking more pride in their properties, what with the city's suburb moving close. Homeowners added or replaced balconies, porches, and roofs.

Daniel found the house. He was hired on the spot! Working with the owner, he carried lumber, reached up boards, and did some nailing. At day's end, Daniel's new boss wiped his brow.

"Come back anytime, Daniel. I'll pay you O.K. money."

"Yes, sir!"

Daniel walked up to the reservoir, feeling great. Near the second turnout, he tensed. A car stood there. The car showed signs of having been rolled over. The roof was dented and the door on the driver's side did not match the faded gray of the body.

Changing to the other side of the road, Daniel noticed Sarge and the black-bearded driver down by the mud flat. They were carrying a sheet of plywood. Their feet made sloshing noises. The skinny teen-ager sat under the cottonwood tree. He was warming himself by a smoldering fire. Sarge called to the teen-ager.

"Hey, Leonard, let's get at that tree before the place dries out and every Tom, Dick, and Harry can get at it."

The sheriff's car passed Daniel. The officer slowed the car, looked over the old jalopy, and went on. He had not seen the men down in the mud.

The three fellows sprang into action below the turnout. Sarge sat on the plywood sheet and the other two pushed him out onto the mud. The sergeant paddled toward one of the skeleton trees. His buddies doused the fire, scrambled up the bank, and jumped into their car. Tires squealing, they raced off.

Daniel walked on. He was nearing Twin Creek when he heard bloodcurdling cries.

"Help! Help!"

The boy turned back, his flesh crawling. Blackbirds chased each other in the low sunlight, shoulder patches aflame. The birds dipped into clumps of grass.

"Help! Help!"

Beyond the birds, a rope hung from the nude limb of a skeleton tree. In throwing it, Sarge apparently had slipped from the plywood raft, and the creek's current had carried the raft out of reach. The sun dipped behind the hills, leaving sudden twilight.

"Help! Help me!"

Daniel did not want to help the sinking man. Mamma's words haunted him: "When someone needs help, we must give it. When somebody's life is in danger, we must give help for free." Daniel cupped his hands around his mouth.

"Hang on! I'll get help." Daniel ran toward the postal trailer. Then he remembered. The post office was closed. The public telephone beside it required a dime (which he did not have).

A car clanked over the cattle guard. It was coming his way. Daniel planted himself in the road. Headlights nearly blinded him. The car stopped and the driver called out, "Is something wrong?"

"A man is stuck in the mud." Daniel recognized the sheriff's car.

"Where?" The sheriff directed a searchlight onto the mud flat. When the bright light uncovered flailing arms, he reached for his CB radio and asked for assistance. He got out and took a rope from the trunk.

"Try to catch that!" the sheriff called, hurling the rope toward the sinking man.

Commuters stopped. "How did that fool get himself into this mess?" they asked. Others answered, "Perhaps somebody had a party and he wandered off. Beer, wine, or drugs, maybe."

Police cars arrived. After much calling and hurling the rope, the officers pulled Sarge to safety. Or was it safety, Daniel wondered? The rescuers asked the mud-crusted man many questions.

"What's your name?" "Who brought you here?" "How did you get out into that mud flat?" "Who do you hang out with?" "Have you been in trouble with the law?" "Have you done time?"

Sarge gave no straight answers. His teeth chattered. A policeman threw a blanket around him. Another policeman spread an oilcloth on the passenger seat and strapped the muddy man into the car. Handcuffed, Sarge was whisked away.

"He was lucky," the sheriff remarked.

"If that boy had not stopped me, he'd have drowned for sure."

"What boy?" one of the remaining policemen asked. The sheriff looked around. "That's strange. He was here a minute ago."

"What did he look like?" the first officer asked.

"He was black-haired, Mexican-American maybe."

Daniel hid behind a bush. He had accepted five dollars from the arrested man. And once he had kept a sealed package for him. Maybe there had been drugs in that package. Sarge had mentioned police once before. Daniel waited until all the cars left. At home, Mamma looked upset.

"Where have you been, Daniel? I worried about you. I thought something happened to you."

"A man got stuck in the mud and I got help for him, Mamma."

"You could get yourself in big trouble on that Reservoir Road, Daniel. Linda says it's a bad road."

"I'm all right. Don't worry about me." Daniel did not feel like eating the supper Mamma had kept warm for him. He was more tired than hungry.

In his bed, Daniel listened for sirens. Why had the sheriff handcuffed Sarge? Had the sergeant been in trouble with the law before? What if Sarge mentioned the sealed package and the five dollars? Would the sheriff come and get him, the Mexican-American boy who foolishly had run for help?

Daniel remembered the blue-jeaned men who fanned out over the road every Wednesday. Young Chicanos were among them. They had been caught. Now they picked refuse under the guard's watchful eye and slept behind bars.

"Dear Lord," Daniel prayed. "Please keep me out of jail, *please!*"

chapter nine

The Trouble with Sisters

After his bad night, Daniel checked the tea in the yard, then headed for his construction job.

Many plants were dying along the road. The poison spray was doing its job. Daniel frowned. A rustle in the shriveled grass startled him. A black cat studied him with yellow eyes. Could she be one of the missing kittens, Daniel wondered? He called her. She bounded off.

A paving truck passed. The trucker waved. Daniel admired the trucker. There was a man who managed.

Sarge's buddies waited for Daniel at the first turnout. The black-bearded driver sat, hairy head tucked into massive shoulders, beside the thin teen-ager Daniel had seen earlier.

"Hey, kid, what happened to Sarge?"

"W-why do you ask me?" Daniel stuttered.

"We saw you on the road last night. Right, Leonard?" The driver turned to the teen-ager beside him.

"Right, Gig." The teen-ager got out. He planted himself in front of Daniel. Reddish hair poured from a frazzled straw hat high on top of his skinny frame. He wiped the back of his hand over his dripping nose as he peered down at Daniel.

"Are you going to tell me or not?"

"I, uh, you have a cold," Daniel stammered.

"Never mind my cold. What happened to Sarge?"

"Police pulled him out of the mud." Daniel wished he could get away.

"Did they drive him away?"

"Uh-huh."

Leonard whistled. He jumped back into the old car. Gig revved the motor and sped away. Daniel adjusted his glasses. The plywood sheet floated on the mud. A woodpecker hammered away halfway up a skeleton tree. A hole gaped in the trunk. A hole! Maybe it was a cache—for drugs. Daniel's ears drummed.

And what about the litter bags the blue-jeaned convicts put beside the garbage cans every Wednesday? Why would Sarge and Leonard search for cans in them? Was there drug traffic going on right under the guard's nose? Were drugs going in and out of the county jail?

"I am being silly," Daniel scolded himself.

Water lapped peacefully at the shore. The surface mirrored brown hills and green oaks. Cows made contented chomping sounds in the pastures, and a ground squirrel darted into the burrow it called home.

Daniel meant to check the garbage cans, but bicyclists puffed uphill and headed for the spot.

At the corral, the colt sprang up at seeing him. It stood beside its mother, long-legged and curious. The mare stood, ears pricked and alert to the boy's presence. Daniel chuckled. The colt's tail was turning round and round.

Construction noises sounded from the churchyard. A saw whined and hammer blows rang out. Daniel hurried on to his own construction work.

The day passed quickly, for Daniel's employer had answers for questions that bothered the boy. The man said that change is part of growing up.

"You want to grow up, don't you?"

Daniel nodded.

And Mr. Randall's friend said not to worry unduly, for God was looking out for people and for sparrows too.

"Without your Father's leave not one of them can fall to the ground."

Daniel repeated the words on his way home.

On top of the hill, Daniel noticed Gig's jalopy on the turnaround. Two girls giggled beside the car. One was blonde and pudgy, the other brown-haired and thin.

Smoke rose from a cigarette the blonde girl was holding. Daniel passed on the far side of the road, thinking of his cousins. He hoped the cousins wouldn't find girls like these. Maybe Gilbert and Emilio had better sense than that. The cousins might be swayed by the pudgy girl, for her hair glowed like honey and her face was pretty. But she might be a bad choice. Daniel had seen her around.

Daniel remembered a girl he first saw on a black horse. She was lovely, the sort of girl he'd want to marry when he grew up.

Papa used to tell him, "Stay away from girls, Daniel. You are too young. Girls can get you in all kinds of trouble, believe me."

Mamma, on the other hand, would say, "When a girl likes a boy, she wants to marry him. It will be many years until you can even think of marrying a girl. When girls get married, they have babies. It costs money to have babies and to raise them too."

The pudgy girl's blonde hair wafted around her shoulders. Daniel contrasted her with the girl he idealized. The girl he remembered had straight hair, glossy and rich. She made this girl look cheap.

What would it take to marry a decent local girl, Daniel wondered? A job, for one thing.

The girl with the black horse lived in a house surrounded by a vineyard. If one wanted to marry a girl like that, one would have to settle down, attend school, and learn a useful trade.

That meant the Morales family would have to stay in one place. Could Papa settle down in one place? Could he do that? Daniel did some hard thinking.

Papa had changed jobs before: gas station attendant, janitor, cement finisher. Could he not attend adult night school in the city? Linda said many Almadeners attended night school in San Jose! Perhaps he should tell Papa about such good opportunities. Linda said night school is cheap. Daniel sat down beside the road, mulling things over.

"Papa does not believe he can learn like other people," Daniel muttered. He sighed. It would be easier to teach a mule to dance than to drag Papa into a school, he feared.

The pudgy girl's giggling broke into Daniel's deep thought. He hoped Linda kept clear of girls like this one. Linda was growing in the Anglo house. Was she safe at the Hendersons'? Daniel watched shadows along a rock ledge. Baby squirrels came out to play. He shaded his eyes against the setting sun. The sentinel saw him. His whistle sent the young ones under the ledge. The young squirrels were safe, thanks to strict supervision.

Mrs. Henderson was strict, Daniel reflected. Despite her smile and baby face, she tolerated no nonsense. She'd keep Linda in the house.

The sun slipped over the hill, leaving twilight. In the half-dark, Daniel noticed spots that moved on the bank. Baby toads hopped over weeds and rocks. The creatures headed for the road!

At the edge of the road, the toads stopped. A few brave ones hopped onto the pavement. Daniel recognized the danger they were in. After their tadpole childhood, the amphibians struck out for life on land. He must help them across the road.

The baby toads hopped back to the bank from whence they came. They were afraid— of him! Daniel planted himself in the road and waited. When the toads were safely across, he let the cars pass.

"Why did you stop traffic?" drivers asked.

"Baby toads are migrating to the hills," Daniel explained. Drivers proceeded with caution. Daniel shuddered, thinking of the toads. What a change awaited the babies! After reaching the hills, they would scatter and fend for themselves, without help from parents or family. The change that had befallen the Morales family was as nothing compared to the challenge the little toads were facing. What gave them the courage, Daniel wondered?

Next day, he asked his employer, who

said, "God watches out for the little toads, Daniel. He watches out for people too. The animals instinctively have faith; that's why they strike out and survive."

During the weeks Daniel worked for Mr. Randall's friend, he got plenty of food for thought. When the last nail was driven, he received his pay and a pat on the back.

"Come back and visit me anytime, Daniel."

Thanks to Daniel's employer, Daniel got new jobs in town as a construction helper. And once in a while, he pulled an envelope out of the mailbox and Mamma found a few dollar bills in it. Papa had not forgotten them.

Daniel was glad, but worries nagged at him too. Angelina no longer begged for a fast ride. She no longer giggled. He'd come home from work and she'd hide behind Mamma. Then Mamma would look sad and say, "She's afraid of you, Daniel. What have you done to her?"

Daniel knew no defense against Mamma's sad brown eyes. He had hurt his baby sister. Efforts to make up ended in crying spells on the part of Angelina.

Linda treated him like ice. "You don't understand me, Daniel," she would say. "You think I am getting spoiled at the Henderson house."

Daniel sighed. Not so long ago, he had

buried his head in Mamma's long hair and she comforted him. Now he felt this empty spot inside him. "I must have faith," he mumbled. "Why, the little toads are smarter than I, for they know how."

The fear that Sarge might get him into trouble added to Daniel's worries. The strange fellow had not come around since his rescue at the mud flat.

One morning, Mamma said the tea was ready for the health-food store. After finishing a construction job, Daniel savored the unhurried morning walk. The reservoir was a steaming cauldron. Night fog sank to the crests of the hills, draping them like bashful brides. Goldfinches fluttered along the roadside. Their yellow breasts matched the blossoms of star thistles, on which they fed.

Always on Monday morning, Daniel ached to tell Linda what he had observed during the week. Linda did not share his love for nature. While he choked up over birds, animals, or clouds, *she* hurried down to the Anglo house.

In school, the teacher had encouraged Daniel to share his observations about nature with the class. Daniel brightened. School had been a good experience. The teacher showed them many fine things. All he, the migrant's son, had to do was sit and learn.

Before summer vacation, the teacher

talked about an artist called Audubon, who painted beautiful bird pictures. She had mentioned a man called Muir, who explored nature and wrote about it. And she had pointed out a writer called Thoreau, who observed nature near a pond. Some day, God willing, he'd read about special people the teacher mentioned and those Mr. Randall's friend talked about. Mr. Randall's friend owned books that told wonderful stories about Bible heroes. Daniel wondered whether his former employer would let him read those books.

An unlikely creature near the shore distracted Daniel. A turtle paddled with clumsy limbs. Somebody had dumped a pet! Daniel was stunned. What a change it must have been for the turtle—from a bowl where people were feeding it to life in open water. Daniel hoped God was looking out for the turtle.

Suddenly, the turtle hid under a floating log. A black cat turned up in the grass. Spotting Daniel, the cat bounded across the road and stopped in tawny oats. Ears turning, she watched him out of yellow eyes, then disappeared. A small mammal whistled where she had vanished. Crunching sounds told Daniel the cat had caught her breakfast. The cat and turtle alike fought for survival. They had faith, for they were not giving up, Daniel judged.

High above the road grew oak trees with roots jutting against the sky. Branches above the exposed roots had withered, but the live side sprouted green leaves. The oaks were surviving and alive. God was watching out for them too, Daniel reasoned.

Daniel set down his tea bags and wiped his face. His shirt was wet between the shoulder blades. The day was going to be a scorcher.

Suddenly, tires screamed around uphill curves, and a car careened into the turn-about. The car went round and round. Wild cries sounded out of the dust cloud it whirled up.

chapter ten

Cattle Thieves

Sarge's jalopy zoomed out of the dust cloud and roared downhill. A pickup truck with two barking dogs behind it followed Sarge.

Soon a bedlam of noises ensued. Dogs barked, a horse whinnied, blue jays screeched, and tree squirrels scolded. Daniel clutched his clumsy tea bags. He did not relish trouble.

Sarge's jalopy and the pickup parked by the horse corral. The dogs were running up the pasture, ahead of Sarge, Leonard, Gig, and a fourth man. They carried sticks or guns. The barbed wire hung loose; it had been cut.

The mare stood trembling in the brush. Her colt jumped up on seeing Daniel. The little horse looked confused and unhappy. The mare's nostrils flared. When Sarge's party vanished over the crest, she led the colt uphill.

"Don't take him up there. Something might happen to him," Daniel warned. The mare flicked her ears, but she kept on going.

Daniel peeked into the bed of the pickup.

A green blanket hid something. Daniel climbed onto the stepside and lifted the heavy cloth. Butcher knives glistened in the sunshine. He dropped the cloth in shock.

Daniel hastened away. Nearing the church, he saw cement trucks, cars, and construction vehicles. Crews of men worked together to pipe cement into the church's basement.

Nobody paid attention to Daniel, or the cows that bellowed over the hill's crest.

Suddenly, hoofbeats rang out on the road. Beyond the cement truck's rotating drum, Daniel spotted the mare. She was galloping onto the highway bridge. Tires screeched. But it was too late! The motorist couldn't avoid the galloping horse.

Daniel put down his tea bags. He must save the colt, so it wouldn't follow its mother. He ran uphill and found the colt—too late. It lay below a cliff, limp and lifeless. Daniel blinked back his tears.

"You should have lived," Daniel sniffled.

Anger replaced Daniel's sorrow. Sarge had chased the horses, or made them panic somehow! Sarge had ruined the mare and killed the colt!

In his anger, Daniel ran up to the corral, only to choke on the exhaust fumes the pickup and Sarge's car were making. Daniel loathed the men's getaway. He turned back and stood guard over the colt.

Men wearing cowboy hats strode up from

where the mare lay, and told Daniel, ''The rancher is saddling his horse. He'll be by soon.''

The rancher arrived on a sturdy horse. He dismounted and felt the colt's body.

''Did you see what happened?'' the rancher asked.

Daniel shook his head from side to side. He did not feel like talking.

''Cattle thieves have been causing trouble around here,'' the rancher told Daniel. ''Last spring, they killed a cow and a calf. They threw the calf into the bushes. The cow they hauled away for meat.''

''Have you—seen those cattle thieves?'' Daniel asked.

''Once.'' The rancher pushed back his hat. ''Last year, when they shot my prize bull. They came with a truck and butcher knives.''

Daniel held his breath. ''Did you—catch them?'' he finally asked the rancher.

''Sort of. The police picked them up, but they got out of jail again. I've lost six cows already and there might be another cow missing right now.'' The rancher pointed uphill.

''What—did the thieves look like?'' Daniel asked. The rancher frowned.

''One was chunky, black-bearded. Another was a tall and skinny kid. The third man wore a padded jacket with sergeant's stripes on the sleeves. I guess he was the leader.''

"Have these men caused other trouble too?" Daniel inquired with caution.

"Who knows?" The rancher sounded upset. "People think, 'What's one cow for a guy who has so many?' Believe me, every head of cattle counts. It's tough to make a living nowadays."

Daniel felt sorry for the rancher, but the words *police* and *jail* stopped him from telling the rancher what he knew about the thieves. The rancher looked at him directly.

"If you could tell me anything you have seen, I'd be obliged to you." The rancher's sharp-cut face looked intense. "These are mean and dangerous men, and anything you have seen might help put them behind bars."

"I, uh, didn't see anything," Daniel stuttered.

The rancher seemed keenly disappointed. He mounted his horse. Riding off, he said, "My men will bring the truck and pick up the colt."

Daniel loathed being caught between wanting to help and protecting his safety. The colt's still body seemed to accuse him.

When the truck arrived, Daniel fetched his tea bags and marched off to the health-food store. He exchanged his harvest for rice, flour, cornmeal, a low-sodium muffin mix for Mamma, and fruity sweets for Angelina.

His arm crooked around the large bag, Daniel marched back to New Almaden. He meant to tell Linda about the colt, but Linda might not understand his grief over "just horses."

Hammer blows sounded at the church. Daniel wiped his hot face in the shady parking lot and watched the action. Four young men worked at upgrading the church. One was up on a ladder, balancing a bundle on husky shoulders. A second man stood on a scaffold, removing crumbly shingles with a long-handled shovel. He tore off the weathered pieces and tossed them from the roof. A third man unloaded new shingles from a truck beside the church's entrance. The fourth man flung a power cable over his head, then ran a power saw over a board along the foundation. He saw Daniel and smiled.

These men were clean-looking fellows, unlike Sarge and his buddies. Daniel remembered Mamma's words: "When somebody needs help, we must give it for free."

"Do you need help?" Daniel asked the men.

"Sure do." They grinned back.

Daniel's offer to help was cheerfully accepted. The men let him put shingles and scrap lumber into neat piles. Daniel bounced over the cushion built up by dry eucalyptus leaves. The men treated him as an equal and Daniel enjoyed working with them. He did not quit until they put their tools away.

"That's it, Daniel. God bless you for helping."

"It was nothing."

Daniel picked up his brown sack from the health-food store, feeling great. The floor was jacked up underneath the church. Wooden forms held in the fresh cement. The little church was no longer falling apart. The next winter's storms would not make the roof leak, or the walls whistle.

The church had stood nearly a hundred years. Its roots went deep into the mining town's history. Growing roots must be a fine thing, Daniel mused.

If one could stay in such a place, one would become part of it! One could share a solid foundation, build on it, contribute a small share, and perhaps be remembered for a worthy deed later on.

Linda's words rang in Daniel's ears. "The people of this town, have they not accepted us? Do they not respect Papa for working instead of drawing welfare? This is a good place to stay, Daniel. If we move on, we must start all over again. We'll be strangers, footloose migrants that nobody cares about. And Mamma, she'll be miserable. No, Daniel, I want to stay here. I want a bed for my babies, not just a dirt heap at the edge of somebody's field."

Daniel heaved a sigh. Linda was going on twelve. She no longer was the girl who used to know nothing. In deep thought, he entered Reservoir Road.

A kingfisher's scream pierced Daniel's

thoughts. The bird sat on a wire above the creek. White neckband, bulky head, stubby tail, exactly like the sketch in the bird book, Daniel reflected. The bird scolded two bushy-tailed squirrels who chased each other over high branches.

He and Linda used to play together, Daniel recalled. He wished he could turn back the clock, wished they were little again. Daniel felt like crying. He had misunderstood Linda. He had hurt Angelina. He had disappointed Mamma. He was barely keeping himself out of trouble. One day, Papa would return and ask how he had kept his promise. Daniel hung his head.

Tires squealed around uphill curves. Without looking, Daniel knew it was Sarge and his buddies. The old car nearly grazed him. It roared past, making the boy's hair stand on end.

Daniel kept on walking in the dusky twilight. If he minded his own business, perhaps they'd leave him alone. The car faced the road with dimmed headlights. Daniel passed the turnout.

No wild cries came from the jalopy. No radio blared. Why the running engine, Daniel wondered?

A jack rabbit start brought the jalopy up from behind. Daniel ran, spilling the groceries in his haste.

"Help me, dear Lord!" he prayed.

The jalopy bucked to a halt. Sarge jumped out. "Get in! I want to talk to you."

"W-who, me?" Daniel's knees shook.

"On the double!" Sarge jerked the backrest and pushed Daniel into the rear seat. "What did you tell the rancher?"

"N-nothing."

"What did he tell you?"

"He, uh, lost some cattle."

"What else?"

"He said every cow counts. It's hard to make a living nowadays."

"Did he say he—saw the cattle thieves?"

"Uh-huh."

"Did he describe—us?"

Daniel nodded, feeling sick.

Sarge uttered profanities. "Let's get out of here!" he told the driver in conclusion. Gig turned the car.

"Let me out!" Daniel pleaded. "My mother worries about me. She has a heart condition."

"Shut up, kid!" Sarge muttered.

Gig was watching the rearview mirror. Two headlights showed behind them. Gig veered from the main road. A wild ride began. The car lurched into curves, headed for rocks, jolted in and out of ditches. Daniel felt relief when a red stoplight came in sight. They were entering the city!

But Gig ran the light, not minding the honking horns of other drivers. A siren started to wail. Gig entered a tree-lined street. They bounced over sidewalks, green lawns, and even scraped a parked car.

Daniel wrapped himself into the pile of blankets on the rear seat. "Dear Lord," he prayed. "Please get me out of this alive."

chapter eleven

People in Trouble

A crunch of metal stopped the ride. The impact flung Daniel between the seat and the backrest. The passenger door flew open, spilling Sarge. Daniel climbed over the backrest and pulled Leonard with him. Gig slumped over the wheel and would not move.

Lights flashed in a nearby house. Voices grew loud. Limping away with Leonard, Daniel saw that Sarge was stirring in the grass. Blocks from the crash, Daniel pulled Leonard behind a bush.

"Why do you keep company with that awful Sarge?" Daniel blurted.

"Sarge cares about me, that's why," Leonard retorted.

"Cares about you? We could have been killed!"

"So what? It beats having a father who's never around when you need him."

"Why, where is your father?"

"Working."

"Is he poor?"

"Poor? My father is a businessman. He makes more money than you've ever seen," Leonard scoffed.

"Then why are you unhappy?"

"'Cause he's never around. He's too busy making money."

"My father is a farm worker," Daniel volunteered. "He hardly makes any money to send home to the family, but he sends all he can." Daniel hung his head. "Papa isn't around when I need him either, but that doesn't mean that he doesn't love me. He loves me very much."

"Mine doesn't like me," Leonard sniffled.

"Nobody likes you with that company you keep," Daniel retorted. "Quit following Sarge and you'll see that your father cares about you a lot."

"But what if he doesn't? Sarge is better company than nobody. You don't know how awful it is to be alone."

"There's still our Father in heaven. He looks out for us. Why, He even looks out for the sparrows."

"Who says?" Leonard scoffed.

"A man I worked for in New Almaden. He's real nice."

Leonard fumbled with a cigarette he had fished out of his pocket. "Have one," he offered. Daniel declined, and suddenly Leonard had vanished in the night.

Daniel hurried away from the scene of the accident. He was lost. Toward morning, he fell asleep in a schoolyard.

Bright sunshine woke him. Daniel adjusted his glasses. One lens was cracked. He noticed it with dismay.

The sound of rattling garbage cans drummed in Daniel's ears. He noticed a garbage truck. It was swallowing the city's refuse. Daniel approached the black man who hoisted a banged-up can onto his shoulder.

The black man grinned.

"You up early, boy."

"Can you tell me how I can find the Almaden Valley?" Daniel grinned back.

"No sweat."

The black man gave detailed directions. Daniel followed the suggested route.

Many intersections and city blocks later, Daniel recognized a shopping center. Then the blue Hummingbird Mountain came into view. He couldn't mistake it, for it had the antenna on top.

Would Linda feed him, Daniel wondered? His feet dragged on Bertram Road. He was dirty and sweaty. Perhaps he could wash up at Mr. Randall's. The drapes were drawn at his friend's house. Noises from the television sounded inside. It was not like Mr. Randall to watch television so early. Daniel fought strange feelings.

"It's me—Daniel," he called.

Something was wrong. Pulse in throat, Daniel opened the door. The television screen flickered. Mr. Randall sat in his chair.

Daniel switched on the light. Mr. Randall looked ill. Daniel fought back his panic.

"What can I do for you?" he asked.

"Call s-o-n-s." Mr. Randall spoke with difficulty.

"Right away."

The numbers of Mr. Randall's sons topped the handwritten directory on the telephone stand. The bottom number was for the ambulance.

"Let p-o-s-t-m-a-s-t-e-r call," Mr. Randall croaked.

"I don't want to leave you," Daniel protested.

"G-o!"

The look in his friend's eyes sent Daniel to the door. Daniel turned back. He kissed the old man's cheeks.

"I love you, Mr. Randall. You've been like a grandfather to me."

Tears streaming from his face, Daniel rushed off to the postal trailer. The postmaster stopped unfurling the flag.

"What's the hurry, Daniel?"

"Something happened to Mr. Randall. Please call his sons. I have the numbers."

Daniel was glad he did not have to make the long-distance calls. Even before the postmaster completed the calls, the ambulance sounded down the street. The postmaster had called that number first.

When Daniel again entered Mr. Randall's

house, the chair stood empty. Mr. Randall's cane had fallen to the floor. Daniel crooked the cane over the armrest, turned off the television set, and left.

Below the highway bridge, Daniel brooded among willows and tules. Bubbles rose from the creek's surface, making peculiar sounds. Mr. Randall was going to die. Daniel knew it deep inside himself. He left the creek, feeling cold despite the sun shining through the willows.

Trucks rolled uphill, still carrying asphalt. A red truck braked on the crest. The scream of its horn startled Daniel. He blinked against the bright sun. The driver waved! Daniel hastened to the truck.

"Hop in!" the trucker invited.

"Thanks." Daniel climbed on the high seat.

The trucker got the big rig going. He was an older man with graying hair and glasses, a grandfatherly type, not burly at all. Daniel felt too tired to let surprises sink in. He meant to ask if there was work for a boy on the road ahead, but all he said was, "Thank you for the ride," before jumping out at the *Dead End* sign.

Daniel reached home, ready to slump into bed. Mamma rushed at him. She looked angry and happy too.

"Thank God you are home! Where have you been?"

"I am sorry, Mamma. I didn't mean to stay away." Daniel couldn't talk about the wild night ride, the long walk, or Mr. Randall's illness just now. Every part of him cried out for rest.

Daniel slept through the day and the next night. The following morning, he devoured his breakfast. Mamma questioned him. Where? What? Who? Why? Her questions never stopped. But Mamma had her share of trouble already. In a rush of emotion, Daniel buried his face in her hair.

"I love you, Mamma. I will be a good boy. Please do not worry about me."

"Está buen, Daniel." Mamma pressed him tight.

Daniel thanked God that Mamma was no longer angry. He hoped she did not worry about him at night. She needed her sleep. He felt sorry to have hurt Mamma and he told her so.

"The colt, Mamma, he fell over the cliff. He was so young. Why couldn't he have lived? And his mother too is dead." For once, Daniel spoke of the colt. Mamma had been close to death once. Surely she must have thought a lot about dying.

"It is better that the colt died, Daniel." Mamma spoke softly. "He could not have lived without his mother. He was too young. If I had died, what would have become of Angelina? She was too young also."

"But now Mr. Randall is dying, Mamma. I'll be losing my good friend."

"Death is part of life, Daniel." Mamma's hand gently brushed over Daniel's hair. "God made it so that nothing gets lost in the world, for when the apricot gets mushy, it will soon sprout a new tree. Mr. Randall has given you good lessons, Daniel. Remember them!"

"But I haven't given him anything!"

"You have given him your love, Daniel." Mamma smiled. "Love is the best thing anybody can give."

"*Gracias,* Mamma." Daniel felt better. Everything was right again between him and Mamma.

"I must get food, Mamma." Even without glasses, Daniel noticed the family's empty cupboards. "Please do not worry about me. I'll be home soon."

On the road, Daniel donned his glasses and hunted for the health-food treasures he had had to abandon when Sarge forced him into his jalopy. Rice, flour, and cornmeal lay spilled over the gravel pile. Only the sturdy box containing Mamma's low-salt muffin mix had remained intact. One of Angelina's fruity sweets turned up in a gulch. Daniel stuffed it into his pocket and hid the box of muffin mix in a safe place.

Daniel hurried on to the postal trailer, where the postmaster gave him a sad nod.

"It's true, Daniel, Mr. Randall died last night. He had another stroke. Sorry."

"Can one . . ." Daniel swallowed, "see him at the funeral home?"

"No, Daniel. Mr. Randall's sons had the body transferred to the East Coast, where they live."

Daniel stood in stunned silence. He wanted to see his friend once more. "Why do things change?" he blurted. "Why can't they stay the same?"

The postmaster pointed to a drawing on the wall. "This is going to be our new post office, Daniel. Just look at that fine new building."

Daniel looked.

"Speaking of change," the postmaster continued. "First we moved our post office out of Casa Grande. Then the post office next door burned down. Then we used the community center. Then we got this temporary trailer. Now look at that new post office. Isn't it beautiful?" The postmaster's arm swept over the sketch. "We'll have a parking lot, flowers, trees, everything!"

"I am glad for you." Daniel spoke from his heart. "Thank you for telling me about Mr. Randall."

Outside, Daniel studied the burned-out ruin next door. It looked depressing. Crumbling adobe walls and charred timbers protruded from the cyclone fence the historical society had put up. Daniel peeked through saplings and tall weeds. Birds whirred in the sunlight, flying and flashing. Lizards scurried over charred planks, and a squirrel flicked its bushy tail on an overhanging branch. Daniel was surprised. The ruin had become a wildlife sanctuary.

At Mr. Randall's house, Daniel opened the gate and gathered up the kittens. Their rough tongues brushed over his chin, they were so glad to see him. He carried the squirming pair through town, beating off barking dogs.

On the highway bridge, Daniel glimpsed the church. Straight rows of shingles climbed up to the ridge, making the new roof glisten. Some changes were for the good, Daniel reflected.

Asphalt trucks still rolled uphill. Truckers held to a brisk pace. Seasoned drivers, they left room for a boy. Daniel admired how the truckers zipped around curves, leaving space for the empty trucks which jiggled downhill. The big rigs never touched the yellow center line.

One of the truckers shifted gears on the upgrade. He slammed on the brakes and caused the trailer to veer. A heavy chain seemed to have come loose under the rig.

The trucker stopped and climbed down stiffly. He was the older man who had given Daniel the ride. The trucker studied the trailer, which angled into the road, posing a traffic hazard.

Daniel stopped a car, while the trucker raised one side of the hood. From the corner of his eye, Daniel saw that the trucker stepped back from the steaming engine and wiped his glasses.

"Do you need help?" Daniel called.

"Thanks, but some buddy will be along." The trucker waved on the driver-education car Daniel had stopped. The teen-age driver skirted the trailer. Harnessed into his seat, he drove under the instructor's watchful eye. Student drivers drove with caution, unlike the wild teen-agers who also used the road.

"You have helped a lot, stopping traffic," the trucker told Daniel.

"It was nothing." Daniel smiled.

Walking uphill, Daniel struggled with the cats. They scared at the sight of an animal at the roadside—a fox. No fear showed in the fox's triangular face. Its ears were pointed and the bushy tail low as it loped across the road. A second fox followed it to a gulch. Then both animals looked down at the boy with the cats. The foxes' coats blended with the hills' gray rocks and golden grasses. Daniel relaxed his grip, and the cats clawed themselves out of his arms.

"Come back!" Daniel chased after the cats, leaving the road just in time to avoid getting hit by what seemed like a runaway rig. He sucked in his breath as he recognized Leonard in the passenger seat—and Sarge behind the wheel. The big rig barreled downhill with the trailer zigzagging over the center line. Driving at breakneck speed, Sarge was bound to slam into the old trucker!

chapter twelve

A Search Party

The crash let Daniel forget about the cats. He ran downhill. The trucker's unhooked trailer had spilled its asphalt. Sarge had crashed into it. Men milled about the accident scene. Their trucks were parked along the road.

"Take it out of gear!" the men shouted.

"It's not going to work."

"Let's get the trailer first."

The truckers detached the trailer from Sarge's rig, laboring to get it out of the road. The sound of a truck horn jolted Daniel. A blue rig towed the old trucker's red one uphill and parked it on a wide spot. Daniel scanned the men. Where was Sarge? Engines growled as drivers braked on the grade. Daniel went from one man to the next.

"What happened to the driver who crashed?"

"Nobody knows," the men replied. "One thing is for sure, this rig wasn't his."

Anger at Sarge welled up within Daniel. Sarge had no respect for other people's lives or property. While men were working to clean up his mess, Sarge was sneaking away in the bushes. And where was Leonard, the foolish teen-ager?

Daniel wound his way past men and trucks. Flares hissed at his feet. The sticks burned red streaks into the pavement. The old trucker stood beside his ruined trailer. Daniel felt sorry for the man. The trucker was having a bad day. He could not fulfill his contract. And now he needed a tow truck and garage work.

"I wish I could help you," Daniel told the trucker.

"Thank you." The trucker looked depressed.

Daniel understood the trucker's plight. Sometimes Papa's pickup hadn't started. The family lost money at such times. Papa was a good mechanic, just as the trucker was a good mechanic. But if a part was beyond repair, it must be replaced. That cost money, for often it meant taking the machine apart in a garage.

Tow trucks hurried up the road. Daniel did not wait around until they hauled away the crippled vehicles. He hastened up the road to find the cats.

The cats did not answer Daniel's frantic calling. Noise and people had driven them away. Daniel picked up the muffin mix at its hiding place and hurried on. Mamma must not worry about him again. A car honked. It carried a silver boat in tow. A man and a narrow-faced blond boy jumped out. They looked at the receding reservoir and asked Daniel, "Where can we launch our boat?"

"Perhaps there is more water left in the lower reservoir." Daniel shrugged.

"Where is that located?"

"Down Almaden to your right somewhere."

"Thanks." The man and his boy drove off. Sadness overwhelmed Daniel. If only he and Papa could go out some day and do something together. Something exciting, such as launching a boat! Daniel hoped the boy appreciated his good fortune.

Mamma greeted Daniel at the gate. She held up a letter. "It was in the mailbox," she explained.

"*Verdad?*" Daniel ripped off the flap on their way to the kitchen. Somebody had laboriously put together a message in English. The scrawl was hard to read. "Papa is coming," Daniel deciphered. "He writes that we must get ready to travel."

"To Arizona?" Mamma's smile changed to a frown.

"*Sí,* Mamma."

"But, Daniel, it isn't time for my checkup yet."

"The person who wrote the letter doesn't

give any dates, Mamma." Daniel checked the postmark. It was smudged.

Mamma looked bewildered. "Daniel, my checkup at the hospital is still a whole month away."

"Do not worry, Mamma. Papa will come in October like he said." Daniel shook the envelope. No dollar bills fell out. Papa had not been able to save money, Daniel guessed. Papa was a hard worker, but he made little money following the crops. Migrant workers did not make money unless the family worked along.

"Maybe I can get something accomplished today," Mamma said. "Papa must find this house clean."

"Let me help you." Like so many times before, Daniel offered to help with housework. But Mamma liked doing things by herself. Daniel understood. She wanted to work. She had worked all her life, from the time she had picked prunes as a toddler to the day heart failure drove her out of the fields. A person so work-oriented could not sit still and be happy.

Mamma had been keeping the cabin clean, but the hot weather sapped her strength. For whenever Mamma overdid, she paid for it with fatigue. Daniel watched her swinging the broom. She had weathered change all right. She was living with that manmade valve clicking inside her heart. How did she do it? He asked her.

Mamma looked surprised. "I thank God for the gift of life and pray I will get stronger."

Daniel sighed. Everybody was coping with change, everybody but himself. He cleaned up the yard, feeling sorry for himself. Angelina did not come out. The fruity sweet still nestled in his pocket. No use offering it to her. She would not take it, not from him.

After the yard trimmings were in a neat pile, Daniel picked up the bucket. He carried creek water to the kitchen. It was part of his daily chores.

The aroma of Mamma's muffins kept Daniel in the cabin. They ate in the growing dusk. Daniel thought that soon now the cabin would get dark in the evenings. After filling the butane tank, paying the rent, and buying food, there never was any money left for the electric bill.

Daniel left the cabin early next morning. He must find the kittens and buy flour and beans. This being Friday, he might ask Linda to carry home the staples in Mrs. Henderson's car.

The morning wind ruffled Daniel's hair. What little water was left in the reservoir glimmered, quivered, and danced with the wind. If he lived a hundred years, he'd not forget this lake, Daniel told himself.

Nearing the dam, Daniel remembered Leonard and Sarge. A helicopter whirred around the cone-shaped hill above the dam. Two cars stood at the turnaround. One was a police car. More police cars pulled uphill and parked along the fence. Voices sounded from the cars. Daniel understood words and phrases.

"Youth lost in the hills."

"Missing person report."

"Narcotics traffic."

"Arrests . . . last night."

A woman sat in the private car. She and a tall, lean man were watching a search party which fanned out over the hills beyond the reservoir. Daniel guessed she was the missing person's mother. The father paced the road. His face was drawn. The mother's face also showed worry lines. Both looked like they hadn't slept all night.

The father approached an officer. "Do you see anything?"

"No." The officer put down his binoculars. He picked up the walkie-talkie.

Daniel felt the parents' agony. He prayed the missing person would be found. The walkie-talkie crackled. A member of the search party asked for directions. The officer consulted a map. It was spread out in the open car trunk. A bullhorn, rope, oilskin, and black boxes showed alongside the map.

The rancher pulled up the road, towing his horse trailer. He stopped and guided the saddled horse down the ramp.

"If we need, we can get half a dozen horsemen together," the rancher informed the officer. He led the horse around the fence, nodded at Daniel, then swung himself into the saddle. Soon he was galloping across the dam.

The sun rose, bright and glaring, over the crest of the hill. The woman in the car donned dark glasses. The lines in her face had grown deeper. Suddenly the walkie-talkie crackled. Excitement charged through the waiting party.

"We have the subject in sight," the voice announced.

A human being appeared on the hilltop. His outstretched arms made him look like a cross against the sunrise.

"Are you all right, son?" the father shouted.

The officer put the bullhorn to his mouth. "Can you hear me?"

The youth waved. Relief washed over the people on the turnout. The officer in charge called off the search party. Several police cars left. The helicopter hummed away.

The first members of the search party became visible on the far side of the dam. The men had braved rattlesnakes and poison oak to find the youth. The father stood at the fence, gazing at the spot where his son had waved. What was going through his mind, Daniel wondered? The officer closed the trunk lid. He turned to the father.

"At least he doesn't seem to be hurt," the officer comforted. Daniel stared. For all his badge and uniform, the officer really *cared*.

The search party, the helicopter pilot, the rancher, all had done their share to find the lost youth. A team of experts had turned out to help the parents find their son. The officer in charge now turned to the mother. She was crying, and he comforted her.

The "subject" arrived with two members of the search party. He was shaking. Daniel held his breath. It was Leonard!

Leonard did not greet his father. He did not hug his mother. The parents who had waited in such agony received no affection now that their son was found. Daniel's face felt hot. Here were three people who had lost the way to each other. He walked up to Leonard.

"Your father worried himself sick about you," Daniel whispered. "Why don't you say 'Hi!'?"

"What if he gives me a bad time?" Leonard's shoulders drooped.

"He won't, you'll see!" Daniel gave the teen-ager a friendly shove.

Leonard stiffened, but he met his father halfway. "Hi, Dad. I'm sorry I gave you a bad time."

The man put his arms around Leonard. Scratchy sounds came from his throat. "I never thought I'd hear you say that, son. Everything is all right now. We'll spend more time together, I promise." He led Leonard to the car.

Leonard was going home with his parents! Daniel wiped at a happy tear.

The walkie-talkie crackled again. "The landowner is bringing down a person who fled the moment he spotted us. This person seemed to be under the influence of some kind of drug. We told him to stop, but he kept right on running and fell or jumped from a cliff."

Daniel sucked in his breath. The rancher rode across the dam. A man's body hung across the saddle behind him. Daniel clutched the wire. It was Sarge! He recognized the jacket. The horse pranced around the fence. The rancher dismounted and pulled the body from the saddle. He laid it, face up, on a gravel bank. Sarge's ice-blue stare glued Daniel to the spot.

"Young man, why don't you tell the officer what you have watched up here? I saw you walking the road, and I saw you come down from my pasture the day all that shooting was going on." The rancher approached Daniel with the officer in charge.

"Who—me?" Daniel felt sick.

The officer planted himself in front of the boy, but he did not look threatening. "You could help keep young fellows like Leonard out of trouble if you told me what you know about this dead man." He pointed to Sarge's body.

"I, uh . . ."

The last members of the search party returned with several sealed packages. "We found these. The dead man must have thrown them away before he ran," they reported. The packages looked similar to the one Daniel had kept for Sarge. That did it!

"I will tell you all I know and show you where I think Sarge has hidden more things," Daniel said. The officer guided him to the police car. Daniel pointed out the hole in the skeleton tree and went out at the pasture gate with its *No Trespassing* sign.

Lo and behold, the two white birds sat high on the oak branch! They spread their wings against each other like stately cherubim. Daniel soaked in the wonderful sight. He'd remember it in his cell behind a barred window, he hoped. The officer saw the birds also. "Look like fish hawks," he said.

Uphill, Daniel found the hump of brown soil, even though weeds had grown over it.

The officer poked a stick into the mound and pulled out the can with the white crystals inside.

Daniel described the plastic marker he had tossed downhill. The officer made a rough drawing. "Did it look like this?" he asked. Daniel nodded yes. The officer slid downhill, braving poison oak. "You stay up here," he told Daniel. "We don't want you to get hurt."

The officer found the marker. Back in the car, he reported his find. Daniel fidgeted in his seat. Would the officer handcuff him? Would he strap him down? The officer put down the speaker. He looked pleased.

"The marker may be a clue. We may need you for further testimony later." He propped up a pad and took down Daniel's name and address. Putting the pad away, he said, "I'll take you home."

"Aren't—you going to take me in?"

"Take you in?"

The officer cupped his warm hand over Daniel's cold one. "Poor kid, you've been scared stiff, haven't you?"

Daniel sniffled. He couldn't speak just now. The officer started the motor. Nearing the cabin, Daniel froze. Two pickup trucks stood beside the creek! Papa had arrived with Uncle Felix! The men must have come over the side road, for Daniel had not seen them pass.

"You can let me out now," Daniel said. "Thank you for the ride."

chapter thirteen

Papa Comes Home

Everything was quiet in the kitchen. Mamma stood by the stove. She was preparing a meal.

"Hush, Daniel. Papa and the relatives traveled all night. I told them to rest. We must wait for Linda anyway."

"Why must we wait for Linda?"

"To get ready." Mamma sounded tired.

"Ready for what?"

"We're leaving tonight, Daniel."

"Already?" Daniel slapped his forehead. "I'll be right back, Mamma. I must find Mr. Randall's kittens."

Daniel dashed off. The turnout was quiet. All the police cars had left. Daniel called the kittens below the dam. The furry creatures wobbled up from the creek and started to purr. Daniel cradled them in his arms. At home, he fed them, and they curled up in a dark corner.

Mrs. Henderson's car pulled up. Linda bounced into the kitchen. She was in a good mood, as always when she came from work.

"How are you, Mamma? How are you,

Daniel? What a good week I had . . ."
Linda rattled.

Daniel stopped her. "Didn't you see the pickups?"

Linda quit bouncing. "I did."

"Don't you know what they mean?"

"Papa is home and Uncle Felix stopped for a visit."

"No, Linda. We're leaving for Arizona."

"You are joking, Daniel."

"I am not. Ask Mamma."

Linda's face changed into a somber mask. Daniel pleaded, "Please don't make a fuss, Linda. Mamma is tired and the one thing she doesn't need is you making a fuss."

Linda put the bagful of leftovers she'd brought from the Hendersons' into the mouseproof refrigerator. She uttered not another word, but helped Mamma with dinner preparations.

Suddenly, the bedroom spilled people: Papa, Uncle Felix, Aunt Lupe, Granny Rosita, Gilbert, Emilio, and Angelina. All seemed rested, except for Angelina, who was crying.

Many greetings and embraces later, the families gathered around the Moraleses' makeshift table. They ate vegetables from Papa's last place of work and chased them with Mamma's spicy beans. Reports of harvests, labor camps, row bosses, and ever-rising prices peppered the meal. Nobody asked personal questions until Angelina acted up. It was Daniel's fault. While passing a dish to Linda, he accidentally brushed against the child. Angelina howled and Aunt Lupe raised her eyebrows.

"What is the matter with the little girl? Is she afraid of her own brother?"

Daniel lowered his head. Leave it to Aunt Lupe to notice a thing like that! Linda came to his rescue. "She gets cranky when she hasn't enough sleep, Aunt Lupe."

"*Ah, si?* The little girl has not spoken a word since we arrived. Can she not speak yet?"

"She lets us know what she wants. We always understand her," Linda defended her sister.

"But she does not *speak,*" Aunt Lupe persisted.

"She speaks when she wants to," Linda countered.

Aunt Lupe changed the subject. "What about your mother, has she made any money this summer?"

Daniel replied for Linda. "Mamma has done her walking every day, Aunt Lupe, and she has been keeping the cabin clean. Perhaps she will find work she can do someday. Many women work in offices, where they can sit all day. Mrs. Henderson, for example."

Aunt Lupe shifted her weight on the fruit

crate. "I seem to remember hearing about *Señora* Henderson," she remarked.

Uncle Felix gave his wife a disapproving look. "Quiet, woman! You talk too much." He faced Daniel. "I suppose my nephew has done a good job being man of the family, no?"

"I, uh . . ." Daniel almost choked on his beans.

"He has, Uncle Felix." Linda answered for Daniel. "He took me down to New Almaden every Monday. I wouldn't have *dared* go by myself."

Daniel gulped. Was that Linda speaking? Mamma fell in with her daughter. "Daniel brought me medicine when I got very ill," she said. "He earned fifty dollars that day."

"Fifty dollars!" Uncle Felix clucked. "What did you do to get so much money?"

"I, uh . . ." Daniel stuttered.

"He didn't do anything," Linda intoned. "Movie people photographed Angelina in the creek."

"In the creek?" Mamma's spoon clinked on her plate.

Linda looked guilty. "I wasn't supposed to tell, but the movie people needed Angelina for a drowning scene. She got wet and scared. That's why she's mad at Daniel, because he gave her to strangers."

Daniel's cheeks burned. He faced Papa. He might as well confess everything. "I am sorry, Papa, but I was a flop being man of the family. I frightened Angelina. I misunderstood Linda. I neglected Mamma. And I didn't even keep myself out of trouble."

"What happened, son?" Papa's Adam's apple bobbed up and down. Daniel showed his glasses. Papa couldn't miss the cracked lens. Daniel spoke of Sarge, Gig, Leonard, and the police.

Nobody interrupted him. Daniel guessed they were too shocked. Papa cleared his throat at last.

"It was wrong for me to leave my family," Papa said. "It was wrong for me to leave you, Daniel. A son needs his father. We won't break up the family again." Papa turned to Linda. "You have helped keep the family apart. You mustn't do it again."

"I didn't know Daniel was in trouble," Linda muttered.

"Está buen, Linda." Papa faced Mamma. "And you, do you want us to part again?"

"No." Mamma shook her head from side to side.

"So it is decided. Rolando Morales and his family, they stay together."

"So we can leave after the meal." Uncle Felix beamed.

Papa waved his brother's statement off. *"Momentino,* Felix. I first must ask my son a question."

"Si?" Uncle Felix looked puzzled.

Papa sat up straight. "Do you want to travel, Daniel?"

"W-what?" Daniel felt rattled.

"Tell the truth, son. Do you think it is best for Mamma to leave this place?"

"N-no." What was Papa getting at, Daniel wondered?

"Do you think it is best for Linda to leave this place? The truth!"

"N-no, Papa."

"Do you think Rolando Morales and his family could stay here?"

"I, uh, guess so, Papa." Daniel felt thoroughly rattled.

Papa now turned to his older brother. "Do *you* think my family should stay?"

"It is no longer for me to decide, Rolando. If your family stays here, Daniel, the oldest, must make decisions some day. He must help his mother, guide his sisters, and take care of you too. How do you decide, Daniel?"

"Who, me?" Daniel was shocked over this turn of events. He did some frantic thinking. If they traveled to Arizona tonight, he'd never worry about police again. He looked around the table. Mamma's quiet face pleaded. She needed the cabin where she could rest when sick. Linda's somber face told him she'd be unhappy as a migrant for the rest of her life. Angelina's curly head peeked out from the folds of Mamma's skirt. The baby had lived like an animal at the edge of a field; she was better off in this cabin also.

"What does my son say?" Papa urged.

Daniel hesitated. Uncle Felix would be angry with him, would he not? "Maybe we better stay, Papa. We are a migrant family. We know how to work together. Maybe this time we can reap a harvest for ourselves."

White teeth flashed in Papa's face. "So it is done. We stay!" he announced.

Uncle Felix, Aunt Lupe, and the cousins looked puzzled. Only Granny Rosita clapped. She had been watching everybody's lips.

"Bravo, Daniel! My husband, God bless him, was a field worker all his life. When he died, Alfredo had nothing to show for his hard work. I am glad you try something better."

"Oh, Granny!" Daniel embraced the old woman. He was so happy that he fetched the kittens, for he knew Granny Rosita loved cats.

Angelina struggled away from Mamma. She headed for the cats. Not minding Rosita, she stroked the purring creatures.

"Look at Angelina," Linda exclaimed. "She never saw any cats before!" A happy grin put sausages under Linda's dancing eyes. Mamma also looked happier than Daniel had seen her look for a long time.

Angelina picked up the cats. She dragged

the furry bundles from person to person, showing them to Daniel last. Words came from the child's mouth.

"Look, Dannel—*cats!*" Angelina was speaking.

Daniel's face felt hot as tears of joy ran over it. His little sister was free from her mute prison at last. His prayer of thanks got jumbled, in English and in Spanish. He hoped God understood.

The relatives left at sundown, but Rosita stayed, to everybody's delight.

Monday morning, Papa took Linda to work. He returned at nightfall, tapping his chest.

"Rolando Morales, he has done many things today," Papa boasted. "He has enrolled the children in school again. He has stopped at the police station, and he has two big surprises." Papa threw out his chest. "Rolando Morales, he is now a swamper."

"What is a swamper?" Mamma sounded alarmed.

"A swamper is the man who cleans up floors, who puts ice in a machine, who services the restroom. A swamper is important, for he gets a paycheck every week."

Papa put on a brave show, for it was not the kind of work he enjoyed doing, Daniel knew.

"That is not all," Papa continued. "The man at the restaurant will buy fresh Mexican food. He will pay for all the food Mamma and Rosita can cook."

"*Verdad?*" Mamma gloated.

Daniel was amazed at how all things had worked together for the good. Change *was* necessary, and it *did* make people grow. He saw his father's white, flashing teeth and his mother's shining eyes. Even Granny Rosita beamed by the hissing gas flame. Daniel felt happy, yet worried.

"What about the police, Papa? What did you do at the police station?"

"They need you for questioning, Daniel."

"Do I have to go, Papa?"

"*Sí,* Daniel. You can help break up a dope ring. Bad people have been selling drugs to young people and getting them into trouble. The kids go out and steal so they can buy more drugs. Many kids get sick or go to jail. Maybe you can help them, son."

"Do I have to?" Daniel wished he had never seen Sarge, Gig, and Leonard. But then, maybe Leonard wouldn't have found his way back to his parents. Something good had come from it.

"You have to, son."

"When must we leave for the police station?"

"First thing tomorrow."

Next morning, Daniel huddled in the cold pickup truck. Gray night fog still filled the canyon. Papa steered around the dangerous curves of Reservoir Road, holding to the narrow strip between shoulder and center line.

Daniel's hands felt clammy. He missed the sun. Only hours from now, it would put the road ashimmer. Daniel sighed. Life, was it not like the road itself, beautiful sometimes, and sometimes ugly? One needed faith to travel such a road. But in the end it was worth it.